Ride to Revenge

Other Avalon Books by Kiz Von Robin

BRONCOBUSTER!
THE RELUCTANT GUNFIGHTER

RIDE TO REVENGE

KIZ VON ROBIN

AVALON BOOKS
THOMAS BOUREGY AND COMPANY, INC.
401 LAFAYETTE STREET
NEW YORK, NEW YORK 10003

PRINTED IN THE UNITED STATES OF AMERICA
ON ACID-FREE PAPER
BY HADDON CRAFTSMEN, SCRANTON, PENNSYLVANIA

To the two solid foundations whose guidance and high standards have enabled me to endure with strength and confidence—my parents.

Chapter One

T HE dust powdered beneath the iron shoes of the black horse. A hot summer sun glared at the sweat-caked coat of the tired beast and heated the felt on the rider's head. Kyle Rivers seemed unaffected by the burning rays as he sat erect and yet supple in the saddle, swaying naturally with the long strides of the horse beneath him. He held his smoldering gray eyes on the far horizon.

A dog barked somewhere in the distance, and then, faintly, like a merry tinkle of far-off bells, childrens' voices drifted across the sage and played on the ears of the rider. Kyle reined his horse to a halt and listened, pinpointing the location of the sound. His eyes looked menacing as they squinted across the rolling hills of sagebrush. Nothing moved in the miles of wilderness under the noonday sun. He nudged the magnificent

1

black into a walk again. Baby dust devils began immediately behind the horse's heels once it started into motion again, and the small whirlwinds, whipped by a sporadic tail breeze, lightly dusted the rider.

The far-off bark of the dog sounded several times, now more aggressive than playful, as it had been at first. Then, as a shot rang out, Kyle lightly touched a spur to his mount and sent it into a swift canter, quickly crossing several gullies and gently rolling hills. He pulled his horse to a stop on the crest of a knoll that gave a full view of a schoolhouse below. A large yard surrounded the building, and thick cedars grew in abundance outside the dusty courtyard, dressing the uneven terrain in subdued green.

Kyle settled his eyes on a scene that reeked of deviltry. Seven men sat their horses while another, who had dismounted, walked toward a dozen small and frightened children who huddled together in a tight group. Four older boys stood near a young woman who was bent over a small boy with a large black and brown dog in his lap.

Quickly, Kyle sent his horse over the ridge and advanced into the yard at a walk, aware that the men had seen him and become tense. They watched him and he watched them. He guided his horse to a point across the yard and pulled up near a covered well. He dismounted facing them, tied his horse, then boldly walked around to the side of the well nearest the men and leaned against it with his arms folded across his chest.

The men watched him for a bit longer, saw that he held his position, then put their attention back on the woman who knelt over the boy and dog. The man on foot swaggered over to them with his heavy batwing chaps flapping in stride. The woman looked up at him and then rose slowly.

"You pitiful, despicable excuse for a man!" she cried.

In one swift motion the man stepped toward her and dragged her into his arms. He skillfully succeeded in capturing a swift, brutish kiss, but the woman retaliated like a wild creature. She squirmed and delivered two quick, stinging slaps that caused him to release one of his arms and shield his face.

The four older schoolboys, who were in their early teens, immediately came to the woman's aid and piled up on the brutal cowboy. She jerked free and the ruckus got into full swing.

At that turn of events, two more cowboys scrambled out of their saddles to help their partner, but Kyle abruptly stood upright, dropped an open palm to his gun butt, and whipped a .45 Colt into play. The revolver quickly obeyed the caress of its master's finger and buried two slugs into the ground in front of the dismounting men. Everyone froze in position. The boys still held the lustful cowboy, but turned their heads enough to look at the stranger.

"Hold yourselves pat, gentlemen," Kyle ordered softly. "Get on with it, boys."

He held the .45 on the group of men as the boys returned to the attack with enthusiasm. Only moments later, the cowboy had had all he could take.

"That's enough, boys. He's down." Kyle directed his next words at the cowboys. "I reckon one of you men better help your pardner to his feet. Then make yourselves scarce."

"Mister, you shouldn't have stuck your nose in here," one of the mounted men growled.

"I reckon the shouldn'ts are in your corral unless it's common practice hereabouts to pick on a woman and a bunch of kids," Kyle answered swiftly.

"You've been warned!" the other man snapped.

A cowboy went to the battered man's aid and helped him to his horse. Then he returned to his own horse and appeared to be mounting. His right hand, slightly hidden behind his body, reached for a gun butt that stuck out of the pocket on his chaps. The move was not missed by Kyle, and he dropped a rigid, open palm down across the hammer, fanning the single action. The revolver spit fire and ripped hot lead through the cowboy's lower arm as he tried to bring the gun around into a firing position.

An eerie silence followed the echo of the repercussion. The injured man dropped his gun and leaned against his horse, holding his arm and emitting whines that could be heard across the courtyard. The cowboy who had spoken earlier spoke again:

"Mister, Bolden will kill you for that."

"I ain't real easy to kill," Kyle answered. "And if I was you, I'd ride before it gets real contagious."

All the dismounted men scrambled into their saddles. Then they turned away in a group and galloped out of sight into the cedars.

The woman dropped to her knees and put a comforting arm around the boy who held his dog. Kyle walked over to the somber group and knelt down beside them. The blond-haired boy looked up at him with muddy streaks on his cheeks where tears followed one after another. His eyes tore a painful path to the bottom of Kyle's heart.

"He shot my dog," the boy sobbed. "He shot my dog!"

Kyle put a strong hand on the boy's tousled hair and gripped his head firmly for a minute. A pain crossed Kyle's face and then vanished swiftly.

He stood up and looked around, and after locating a bucket near the schoolhouse, he picked it up and carried it to the well. From the wooden well bucket, he filled the bucket with water for his horse. He lowered the bucket on its rope and dipped up another pail of water from the cool depths of the well, balanced it on the edge, and then took a metal dipper from a peg on the side of the well and dipped it in. As he put the long-handled cup to his lips, his eyes rested on the young schoolmarm who came across the yard toward him. She was a brown-haired woman whose beauty he appreciated though he didn't allow any of that appreciation to show on his face.

"Thank you," she said. "I don't know what we would have done if you hadn't come along."

Kyle lowered the cup and refilled it. He studied her brown eyes for a moment, then raised the cup and looked over her shoulder at the older boys, who stood watching him.

"You'd have done all right. Those boys are worth their salt."

"You like youngsters," she said, smiling pleasantly.

"I reckon," he whispered. The anger intensified in his eyes while he drained the cup. "Thanks for the water. Good day, ma'am," he said, tipping his hat.

"My name is Karen McLaughlin. I'm the teacher for the farmers. You're not with the cattlemen, are you?"

"Meaning . . . ?"

"Well, there are cattlemen here and there are also farmers. I hope you're not with the cattlemen, though you don't look much like a farmer."

"I'm not with anyone, ma'am," Kyle said.

"If you're looking for work, I know men who need good hands," she said, following him as he went to his horse to mount.

"I'm not looking for work," he said as he swung into the saddle.

"If you're just drifting, this country could use more good men. This is an excellent land to settle in."

"I'm not drifting, ma'am," he said. "I'm looking."
He reined his horse around her and moved it out across
the courtyard to where the boys stood. "Where's the
nearest town?" he asked the tallest of the group.

"About ten miles east. You'll cross a river about
six miles from here, and watch for the quicksand holes.
Mister, what's your name?"

"What's *yours?*" Kyle asked.

"Simeon Schweeney. What's yours?"

"How old are you, Simeon?"

"Fifteen. Aren't you gonna tell me your name?"

"My friends call me Kyle," he said softly.

For a while, Kyle watched the small boy continue
to stroke the head of the dead dog. Then, looking
grimmer than ever, he headed away from the school.

The black horse bore him swiftly to the river, and
he soon found a place where the water was rushing
over rapids with rocks lining the bank on each side.
He put the horse into the water and crossed safely.
About four miles farther on he emerged from dense
cedars and gazed at the town nestled against a hill. A
large formation of rocks rose abruptly on the bluff
behind the town. Beyond that, spiraling ramparts of
snow-covered peaks glittered in the late-afternoon sun.

Kyle nudged his horse onward. He passed a sign
that named the town as Cedar Point, and he kept alert
as he walked his horse onto the wide main street. He
rode through the town, made a mental picture of what
was there, then circled his horse around the outside

and came back in the direction he had entered. After taking his horse to the livery and seeing to its comfort, he threw his saddlebags over his left shoulder and quietly blended in with the busy little town's residents.

He located a boardinghouse that offered three meals and a bath and checked in. It was late in the evening when he stepped out of the boardinghouse onto the boardwalk, belly full, void of trail dust, and smelling much better than when he'd gone in. He walked a short way along the boardwalk, found an empty chair a few doors down from a saloon, and eased himself into it. The town buzzed with life as Kyle Rivers watched. That was what he had done for the last two years . . . watched.

Quite soon it became evident that the saloon catered to the cowboys. The schoolmarm had said that this was also an area of farmers, but Kyle failed to see a single farmer enter the saloon. After an hour or so he noticed several men who weren't cowboys enter a doorway across the street, and he got to his feet and strolled in that direction. A general store bounced yellow light off its wooden floors and flooded the night air for several feet into the street. Kyle studied the interior from out on the walk without stepping into the light.

About a dozen men sat around a stove and sipped from jugs or drank from tin cups. He saw a big black-bearded fellow get up and go to the stove, fill his tin with coffee, then return to his chair.

Kyle entered the store, where there was suddenly a

cold silence. He walked to the counter in the back near the seated men and leaned against it, facing the group. A man stood up and addressed him:

"I'm usually closed this time of night, but if you have an emergency, I can oblige you."

"Just looking for a cup of coffee and good company," Kyle said.

"If Bolden sent you to eavesdrop, tell him to go chase his tail," a man muttered.

"Easy, Gus," the big bearded man said. "He looks only about half cowboy. Who are you, stranger?"

The big man's speech was broken by rolled *r*'s, and all his *w*'s sounded like *v*'s. Kyle knew the man to be German.

"I'm a man that don't know any cowboys hereabout nor any farmers, but I prefer coffee and the company that goes with it over what I'd find in the saloon."

The bearded man scrutinized Kyle for a minute, and then turned and walked over to another counter. He leaned over with his belly across it, fumbled beneath the back side, and came up with a cup. He went to the stove, filled the cup, and then extended it to Kyle.

"Come over and sit down. There's plenty of chairs."

Kyle accepted the cup and found himself a seat. The looks from the men were all distrustful except for the storekeeper and the big German. Kyle sipped the brew and ignored the looks. He peered solidly at each man as his attention swung around the circle.

"Your little town feels a bit touchy," he said.

The silence continued as the men pursued unfriendliness, and no one chose to answer his comment. Kyle had almost finished the cup of coffee before the German spoke:

"My name is Rolf Schweeney. What's yours?"

"Kyle Rivers," he answered, then saw the resemblance between this man and the boy at the schoolhouse. "I met a Simeon Schweeney a couple of hours ago. Any relation?"

"My son. Where'd you see him?"

"At the schoolyard. He and three other young fellows were whipping the pants off a cowboy that wasn't real respectful toward their schoolmarm."

Immediately, the unfriendly atmosphere in the store changed to questioning curiosity and exclamations chased by a few grins.

"By cracky, I'd have given ten bags of spuds to have seen that," a thin, redheaded Irishman said with a chuckle.

Rolf Schweeney didn't comment, and frowned down at a knothole in the wood flooring. The remarks around the circle quieted down when it became apparent that Schweeney didn't share the enthusiasm.

Kyle reprimanded himself inwardly for mouthing off. Not all men admired violence, whether it was called for or not. In Kyle's opinion, the boys did the right thing, but Schweeney might be a man who would punish his son for fighting.

"Aw, what's eating you, Rolf?" the Irishman inquired.

"I cannot admire my son being the fourth man beating up on one. This will not end here. By our patience and lack of violence we have managed to exist in this valley. We agreed long ago not to band together like an army, but to fight on our own ground for our own possessions. I fear no man, but neither do I invite trouble. Bolden will retaliate if it was one of his men."

A man had entered the store and listened to Rolf's comment about the scuffle. He came forward into the light, and Kyle noticed that most of the men around the circle nodded to him.

"Excuse me, Rolf," the man said, "but I came into town to tell you about that very thing. My son told me that there were eight men at the school today and one of them shot little Danny Brown's dog just for the heck of it." The man turned his attention on Kyle. "Are you the man that held a gun on the rest of the rowdy cow chasers after they tried to maul Miss McLaughlin?"

Most of the men voiced angry protests at what they'd just heard. Schweeney held up his hand and the group quieted. He turned his attention to Kyle.

"Are you the man?"

Kyle glanced around at the angry men. What he said would fuel or choke the fire of fight in these men. He put his attention back on Schweeney.

"Only one man attempted to lay a hand on the lady,

and that man was called a pitiful excuse for a man by her. I don't agree with his actions, but the man was insulted in front of his pards, and her words probably forced him to react the way he did.''

"Are you standing up for him?" asked the man who had just joined the group.

"No, I'm just saying that if you get all huffed up over this incident, you better know that the other side might have a different point of view.''

"Don't you think the varmint a pitiful excuse for a man if he shot a little boy's dog?" the newcomer demanded.

"I reckon, but there's a thing called wisdom and the lady didn't use much of that. A lack of that is especially destructive when it's teamed up with an overabundance of spunk.''

"I doubt that one man holding a gun on eight could be considered using wisdom," the man answered.

Kyle looked down into his cup. He considered a sharp, insulting answer, but he stifled it and planted a look on the man that caused him to back up a step.

"I reckon the eight executed a lot of wisdom by not drawing on me." Kyle stood up and walked over to the counter. He put the cup down, then nodded at Schweeney. "Thanks for the invite. That was good coffee.''

Kyle turned his back on the group and strolled out into the night. He saw the flash of a star on a man's vest when the man passed the lighted saloon and stopped to glance in a minute. Kyle quickly crossed the street and took up a chair on the boardwalk in front of a small newspaper office. He again watched the town.

It appeared to Kyle that the country was on the brink of a range war. He had seen a lot of this, the usual push by the cattlemen to oust the farmers from homestead lands. In this town, nothing had yet flared high enough to cause it to break into a hot war. He thought about the incident in the schoolyard and what might come of it, and then he put it out of his mind. He wanted no part of it, nor did he intend to stay here more than a few days. Next, he let his mind wander into the past, and touched the scar on his wrist where an iron bracelet had cut him cruelly. His eyes smoldered in anger in the darkness until he forced himself to concentrate on the town again.

A group of horsemen came down the street at a steady trot. They dismounted at the hitching racks near the saloon and then entered the establishment. A voice called out to one of the men as he stepped through the swinging doors:

"Mr. Bolden, good to see you. Step right up here and have one on me."

Kyle straightened up in his chair and listened intently, but he heard no more as loud laughter and talking barged out into the night air. He got to his feet and made his way across the street, watching for the lawman he'd seen earlier. Then he took a position near a window that cast yellow light out onto the walk.

Bolden was plainly distinguishable inside thc establishment. Cowboy after cowboy tried to buy him a drink, but the man declined every one and bought his own. The cattleman was fairly tall, and streaks of gray showed at his temples. His jaw was square and his features stern, but he appeared congenial with everyone. Suddenly Kyle saw him pull his revolver from the holster, rap loudly on the bar, then turn and face the men in the saloon as hc slipped the gun back into the holster. It became quiet immediately.

"Perk up here, neighbors. We got ourselves a problem," Bolden said. "It appears the farmers have hired themselves a gunman. There ain't been any trouble here, us being so patient and all, but I figure that must have been an error on our part, 'cause now they've pulled a fast one on us."

Kyle heard rumblings drift out as the cattleman waited, letting his words soak in. It became quiet again and he continued:

"I figure Jory Breene, Henry Tritch, and Rolf Schweeney are the ringleaders in this. Schweeney's boy led a gang of grown boys down at that farm schoolhouse and beat the stuffin's out of my foreman after he shot a rabid and dangerous dog. That hired gun kept the rest of my men pinned down in the brush and managed to shoot one of my cowboys through the arm. They didn't know how many farmers were with him, but they didn't dare risk popping their heads up. My foreman managed to get to safety, and they barely escaped with their lives. Now don't you men think it's time we quit being nice?''

The saloon was quiet except for the few enthusiastic outbursts that came from Bolden's men. The cattleman looked around at his neighbors and frowned.

''What's the matter with you? Do you want every inch of grazing land plowed under by these crooks? If we don't stop them now, they're gonna drive us out so there's room for more of them!''

''Bolden,'' a tall cowboy drawled, ''I don't agree with you on your opinion about the ringleaders. I don't doubt you've got good proof of the hired gun, but I don't believe for a minute that Rolf Schweeney would be a party to hiring a gunfighter.''

Several men nodded in agreement to that. Then a cowboy with two purple eyes and several other bruises on his face stepped in front of Bolden and addressed the crowd. Kyle immediately recognized the man who had kissed the schoolmarm.

''Just look at my mug! You fellers are blind as a bunch of bats! I went over to make sure that mad dog was dead, and that danged gunfighter ordered those boys to jump me. *He's* giving the orders now, and Schweeney's boy was in the lead!''

Kyle had heard enough. Bolden and his man were lying, and whether Bolden himself didn't know the truth or was in on the lie didn't make a difference, because they were using Kyle's actions to attack the farmers. Most cowboys were honorable, but not this

man of Bolden's. Gambling on the integrity of the rest
of the cowboys in the saloon, Kyle stepped through
the swinging doors.

He couldn't watch his back no matter where he
planted himself, and therefore he strode up to within
a few feet of the man with the iridescent face. Not a
chair scraped or a man coughed. The silence that had
descended near the door when Kyle entered the saloon
now spread across the room like an epidemic.

Bolden recognized something about Kyle's carriage
that warned him to tread softly. Kyle put a smoldering
eye on the foreman, dismissed him as of no importance,
and rested the same smolder on Bolden.

"Mind if the other side is told?" Kyle said.

"What side is that, and who are you?" Bolden demanded.

"I'm the man that's gonna send your foreman down
to chat with Satan unless he coughs up the truth!"

Whispers and mumbling went on around and in back
of Kyle. He ignored the fragility of his position and
pushed where he had the strength to do so. He put his
attention on the foreman who stood only feet from him.

"Did you shoot little Danny Brown's dog just for
the heck of it?" Kyle asked softly.

"'Course not," the foreman answered.

"Did you manhandle the schoolmarm and force a
savage kiss on her?" Kyle asked in the same soft tone.

"'Course not," the man said again.

"Any chance the boys already had you dog-piled before I got into it?"

"No. You ordered it."

"And is there any chance I was the only man standing in the open the same as all eight of you were and you all obediently left at my request?"

"Heck, no," the foreman said.

"You're a bald-faced liar."

The cowboy turned even more purple in the face, glanced around nervously at his boss, then looked Kyle in the eye. Kyle stepped back a couple of steps and let his hand drop down near his gun butt. The cowboy had not seen Kyle draw out at the schoolhouse, but the other men had told him it was too fast for any of them to take on. The foreman sweat and bit his lip. He glanced at his boss again, then back at Kyle.

"She insulted the life out of me," he said quietly.

"And I would have agreed with you on that," Kyle said. "But since you lied about every bit of the rest of it, I reckon I agree with what she said, that you're a pitiful, despicable excuse for a man."

Kyle wanted the man to draw on him, but the man looked down at the floor and avoided his eyes.

Kyle knew he had made his point with the men in the saloon. He shot a disgusted look at the man he faced, turned, and walked toward the swinging doors.

"Look out!"

In almost the same instant that the hoarse voice yelled its warning to Kyle, he twisted and rolled to the floor, drawing his .45 as he fell. A shot went just over his head and out under the swinging doors as Kyle squeezed the trigger and sent a deadly message through the man's heart. The foreman's gun flung out of his hands as the impact slammed his body against the bar. He slumped down onto the tobacco-stained floor and lay still.

Kyle regained his footing, picked up his hat from where it had fallen, and continued on out the door. He stepped into the night, saw the lawman running down the boardwalk, and quickly melted into an opening between two buildings.

An hour or so later Kyle slipped quietly into the boardinghouse and went to the long room full of beds. Several men burned lamps by their beds, and they glanced at Kyle when he entered, but otherwise he was ignored. Apparently the lawman hadn't raised much of a stink about the shooting.

Kyle pulled off his shirt. He unbuckled the heavy gun belt and hung it over the bedpost along with his hat. Then he sat down and pulled off his boots. With his hands behind his head, he lay in bed and stared at the dimly shadowed rafters overhead.

He hadn't intended to kill anyone, but such things had been happening in the last two years, and he could only blame it on his inner anger. The fact that he was fast on the draw also made him boldly confident, and he found himself pushing situations that a man would normally avoid. He continued to question his actions, but then a curtain seemed to lift and the tear-brimmed eyes of little Danny Brown were staring at him. Instantly Kyle knew that what had happened tonight wasn't accidental. It was as if Danny Brown had needed somebody to fight for him because of the dog, and somehow Kyle had taken on being that somebody. But he didn't know why.

Suddenly the door to the long, narrow room opened and the lawman stepped inside and closed the door behind him. He looked directly at Kyle, saw the gun belt hooked over the short bedpost under Kyle's hat, then advanced and sat himself on the bed across from Kyle.

"You the man that did the shooting tonight?" the sheriff inquired softly.

Kyle studied him without answering, trying to figure out his game. If the lawman didn't know he had done it, why was he here?

"You'd do well to answer me, stranger. I'm not against you yet. It'd be wise to keep it that way."

Kyle continued to study the man without answering. He hated the law with a passion. It had done him an injustice he refused to forget. The sheriff continued:

"I don't know what's got you clammed up, but rest easy about what happened tonight. The cowboys cleared you. Johnny drew first and tried to shoot you in the back. Even Bolden verified that."

"Then what do you want with me?" Kyle demanded, unable to keep the bitterness out of his voice.

"Did the farmers hire you?"

"No."

The sheriff stood up and gave Kyle a long look. He reached over and tossed the hat down on the bed near Kyle's head, then lifted the gun belt off the bedpost.

"There's enough hate in your voice to scorch me down into a grease spot, mister. I'll hang this on the door latch when I leave. From what I've been told, you're a gunfighter, and from the cut of this holster, it looks to be true. If you're looking for action, don't stop here, and don't ignore my advice, because I can give you more trouble than you can stand. Take my word for it."

The lawman walked over to the door, hung the gun belt on the inside latch, gave Kyle a parting look, and then quietly closed the door.

Kyle got off the bed and retrieved his gun belt. Then he lay down again. But this time he slipped the .45 under the pillow. He glanced around and saw the men looking at him, but they quickly averted their gazes and wisely went on about their own business.

Chapter Two

A STORM rolled in during the night and Kyle awoke to the sound of rain on the roof. But the wetness was not limited to the outside. A cold drip from overhead dashed itself into a spray on the pillow near his ear, its coldness rousing him in the predawn hour. He swung his feet over the edge of the cot and felt the bed next to him. No one was in it and it felt dry. He changed beds and tried to go back to sleep, but sleep eluded him, and so he slid into his shirt and boots, buckled on his gun belt, crammed his hat down on his head, and left the sleeping room.

A light glowed in the kitchen several doors down the hallway, and he ambled to the doorway and looked in.

The schoolmarm he had seen the day before was stirring a large pan full of something. After adding

21

more ingredients, she stirred the mixture as if she were mad at it. She didn't see Kyle step through the doorway and seat himself on a chair near the stove. She didn't look up from her task, and he watched her while she stirred.

Kyle could barely contain a grin as he watched her hips stir in the opposite direction of her shoulders. He folded his arms and leaned back in the chair, totally entertained.

About that time she looked up, gripping the pan in one hand and smoothing a stray strand of hair back under a dust cap with the other. She jumped, recovered quickly, and gave him an indignant look.

"Please don't stop on my account," he said.

"How long have you been there?" she demanded.

"Miss McLaughlin, I'll bet you can dance up a storm."

"And I'll bet I won't put up with you much longer if you don't wipe that ridiculous look off your face," she threatened.

He sobered and glanced at the stove, where a coffeepot puffed steam through its spout.

"Coffee ready?" he asked.

"Not quite."

"Can you put up with me long enough for the coffee to get done?"

"I suppose."

"I thought you were a teacher."

"I am, but on Saturdays I relieve the cook so she

can have some time off to take care of her family. I doubt the boarders would put up with closing the kitchen for a day. Did you decide to stay a while?''

"No," he replied. "Is there a man in the area by the name of Jeb Grosse?"

"No. If he were in this area I would know, because I handle the ballots in the town elections. Why?"

"Just curious," he said and looked at the coffeepot.

"Not ready," she said, putting down the mixture and covering it with a flour-sack towel.

"How long have you lived here?" he asked.

"Four years."

"Do you know of a blond-haired man with a scar across his face?"

"No. Not that I recall."

She poured a cup of coffee, handed it to him, and smiled briefly. Then she went to a cupboard and began pulling pans out.

"The boys said your name was Kyle. Do you also have a last name?" she asked without looking at him.

"Name's Rivers, ma'am." He savored the hot brew as he watched her hands at work. "How's the little guy handling the death of his dog?"

"He's taking it real hard, because life has been hard for him and the dog was about the only thing that had gone right. It isn't fair."

"Why has it been hard on him?"

"He's an orphan. Well, not really. The widow down at the cottonwoods took him to raise from his mother.

The woman just dumped him, as I understand it.'' The schoolmarm looked up at him as she made a quick trip from the stove to the cabinet. "Mr. Rivers, I hate to seem rude, but I need to get breakfast ready. The boarders will be down in a little while.''

Kyle drained his cup, placed it on the kitchen table, and excused himself. He walked out of the boarding-house into the street. The dull glow that pried through the clouds in the eastern sky announced the coming of the sun. The rain had stopped, but the downpour had left the streets looking like a hog wallow.

The general store, down a ways and across the street, was already open for business. Even though the morning had not come to full birth, many people were out on the town's boardwalks. Kyle saw that there was no way to avoid the mud and stepped off into the street. He paused on the other side and sat down on the edge of the walk and cleaned off his boots with his pocketknife.

Inside the store, the ring of chairs was empty except for the Irishman who had been there the night before. He nodded to Kyle when he entered the store. The proprietor reached under the counter for a cup. He slammed it down on the counter with a bang that made Kyle and the Irishman both jump. The man grinned.

"Wanted to make sure you were awake," he said, then shoved the cup toward Kyle. "Coffee's hot."

Kyle took the cup and filled it from the pot on the huge stove. He eased himself down into a chair across from the Irishman and slowly sipped, watching them passively.

"My name's Jory Breene," the Irishman said. Then he nodded toward the proprietor. "He's a mean old geezer by the name of Henry Tritch."

Tritch frowned. He wasn't a big man, but his frame had a tough and wiry look to it. He came around the counter with a cup in his hand and filled it. He frowned at Jory Breene again.

"You always expect the worst in a man and you always get it," Tritch said. He turned to Kyle. "I was informed that you were very active in the saloon last night. There hasn't been a killing in this town in two years. I hope you aren't planning to make a habit of it."

"I don't plan to stay, so rest easy."

"What are you doing here, anyway?"

"I'm looking for somebody."

"If the look in your eye is any indication as to your business with that somebody, I'm glad I ain't him."

A tall, lean, hungry-looking man moseyed into the store. He brought his own cup, stood sipping from it after he had filled it, then turned to go without having spoken.

"When's the funeral?" Breene asked, his voice halting the man.

"Bolden said he'd be in town just before noon. I'll have the hearse ready by eleven," the man answered. He squinted at Kyle and looked him up and down.

"Reuben Sparks, meet Kyle Rivers," Tritch said. "Kyle, Reuben's our local undertaker."

"I got a feeling you're gonna be my next customer, Mr. Rivers. I better get to work on a coffin to fit your carcass." Without a backward glance, the undertaker strode abruptly from the store, not waiting for Kyle's answer. Kyle raised his brows and looked at Tritch.

"The sheriff had a heck of a time quieting down Bolden even though he admitted that it was self-defense on your part," Tritch said. "And Rube probably figures that means Bolden will have it in for you." Tritch looked thoughtfully into his cup. "Getting on the wrong side of Bolden wasn't wise, Rivers. It's good you're moving on."

Breene spat angrily, "I've been on the wrong side of Bolden ever since I can remember, and there ain't a doggone thing stupid about it!"

"You've been lucky," Tritch told him. "And you've been able to keep up your hotheadedness because you don't have a family. Your brother left this valley the same as many others because Bolden used their families as weapons against them. Perhaps I should put it differently and say that it isn't wise for a man with a family to cross Bolden."

"Perhaps you should say that you've all forgotten how to fight," Breene snapped.

"Jory, we don't want to fight. In this land, a man has the opportunity to live in peace, and that's what we're working toward. We don't want a war with Bolden!"

Jory Breene got up and stretched, eyeing first Tritch and then Kyle. He glanced through the open doorway into the sunlight outside, and when he spoke, he allowed his gaze to linger in the street. "Well, you're gonna have to fight. You're all ignoring something that's screaming in your faces, and when you finally take the plugs out of your ears and listen, you can count me in."

Breene took his cup to a wooden stand with a basin and water bucket and he dipped a dab of water into his tin, sloshed it around, and dumped it into the pan. He put his cup under the countertop and nodded to them as he left.

Tritch let out a breath of air that whistled through his lips. He looked at Kyle and shrugged, saying, "Jory likes to scrap. He figures that entertainment at a family reunion should be a bloody brawl."

"I like scrapping too," Kyle said. He drained his cup and walked over to the wash pan. "Especially when it involves a man who has the power to hurt people and ain't got any more right to do so than the next man . . . kinda like Bolden. No, Tritch, I figure there's a time for violence. But maybe you're right, it needs to be left to those who don't have to worry about a family. Then again, a man without a family has nothing to lose but neither has he got as much reason to fight. Thanks for the coffee."

"Just a minute," Tritch said quietly.

Kyle hesitated, watching as Tritch thoughtfully rolled his coffee cup around in his hands.

"Did you purposely badger Johnny so you could gun him?" Tritch asked without looking up.

"You think I badgered him just so I could kill him?" Kyle growled.

"I know you badgered him, and so do a lot of other folks."

Kyle adjusted his hat and stared out through the open doorway into the dusty street. When he looked back at Tritch, the man was gazing intently back at him.

"You think I planned to hunt him up and badger him till he fought back just because I wanted to gun somebody?" Kyle inquired.

"Any other reason?"

"Probably not," Kyle said. "Unless it would be a look I saw in a little boy's eyes. Naw, it couldn't be that," he finished scornfully.

Kyle strode out of the store, angry at himself for giving Tritch an answer. He hadn't intended to make any acquaintances when he rode into town, but somehow things had just rolled along and he felt a kind of friendship with the men he'd briefly met in the store. Tritch's inquiry or insinuation, whichever it had been, said that they considered him a cold-blooded killer, and maybe he was. The thought shouldn't pain him, but it did. He returned to the rooming house.

The dining room was fairly filled for breakfast, and most of the boarders were almost finished when Kyle pulled up a chair and asked for the eggs. There had been a moment of tenseness after he entered and seated himself, but when he broke the silence, the conversation continued around the table.

Karen constantly rushed in and out of the kitchen to refill the platters. Kyle ate slowly and watched her, sure that she could dance well.

"When's the burying?" somebody asked.

The inquiry was answered from down the table: "Around noon."

"Reckon we'll all get a look at Queenie since it's her foreman we're gonna be plantin'."

This last remark made Kyle curious, and he glanced at the stout speaker, but he had enough range etiquette in him not to ask questions. After a moment the man shot a grin at him and then offered an explanation:

"We all call Mrs. Bolden that, because she's so blasted bossy. Bolden used to run his own spread until she came along. The old man wasn't nearly so rotten to folks until she barged in and started calling the shots."

Kyle nodded and continued with his meal. Karen stood stiffly near the kitchen door, listening to the men talk. A disagreeable look appeared on her face.

"Just so you don't make any more mistakes, stranger, Queenie Bolden is the one to watch out for. She was married to Bolden's stepson, and then the son died of the fever and Queenie ups and marries the old man, hoping to get her fingers on the ranch. But the joke was on her 'cause Bolden didn't tell her that his first wife actually owned the ranch and had left the entire spread to her son. Queenie inherited it without having to marry Bolden, but she didn't know that until after Bolden tricked her into marrying him so he could get it back. Serves her right. She's a beast.''

"*Mr. Brownlin!*" Karen said crisply. "You will please not bounce around a lady's good name and honor in this place, let alone in my presence. Gentlemen should keep such things hushed!''

"In all due respect to you, Miss McLaughlin," the man retorted softly, "we needn't be preached at concerning our duties as gentlemen. Stick to teaching boys, ma'am. As you can see, we're all out of school and, in conclusion, I might add that we have never bounced around a lady's name unless you mistakenly place Queenie Bolden in the same category as other ladies. Now if that offends you, I will take my punishment and be more than glad to stay after today's lesson and spend some moments alone with you, Miss McLaughlin.''

A subdued laugh rumbled around the table as Karen's cheeks reddened. She lifted her chin and smartly walked over to Mr. Brownlin, but not close to him.

"It is plain to see that you were denied the opportunity to partake of the polish and education that becomes a gentleman, Mr. Brownlin!''

A roar of laughter sounded as Brownlin got several good slaps across the back. The giant of a man grinned at the comments. Karen smiled and tossed a small towel at him. As she walked back into the kitchen, she told him, "Here, see if you can rub some of that tarnish off and bring out some shine, Mr. Brownlin."

Kyle stopped eating and gazed through the opening to the kitchen where she had disappeared. The women were few and far between who could take a chewing, half an insult, a little teasing, and a lot of general rowdiness from a bunch of men and end up lightheartedly throwing it back in their faces without showing hurt or anger. That admirable trait in her drew deep thought from him for a moment, and then he returned to finishing an excellent breakfast.

Under a noon sky, Bolden's foreman was placed into the deep, cool darkness of the earth. The procession that gathered at the cemetery was of an admirable size, but Kyle, who observed it from a covert position, often heard laughter and joking rather than the usual mourn and weep of a funeral. Apparently Johnny didn't leave a lot of friends behind. Bolden and his men attended, but the queen Kyle was curious to see didn't show. He walked back to the nearby town with Jory Breene and the good-natured Brownlin.

"Did anybody say why the queen didn't attend this burying of Johnny?" Brownlin asked Jory.

"Nope."

"Seems strange, doesn't it? I can't recall her not responding to an opportunity to cuss and scream at us. I wonder what kept her home?" Brownlin shook his head as if he couldn't understand. "I never saw a woman that took such a fancy to running men and bawling them out. If Bolden didn't let her hold the reins, she'd probably have him shot.''

"Guilty conscience," Jory quipped, watching the road ahead of them.

"How do you figure that?"

"Nothing makes anybody so mean as knowing they made a mistake and having to live with it and not being able to. I'd say that she tried to take the reins from a good man and lost him over it. That'll make a woman as bitter as all get-out, but that kind will never admit it.''

"Kinda makes Karen McLaughlin mighty special, don't it?'' Brownlin murmured half dreamily.

Jory testily scrutinized the stout man who was twice his size. "Brownlin, don't go getting sweet on the teacher. We need her here. She can get along with the cattlemen *and* the farmers, besides being the best teacher we've ever had, and the best looking.''

Brownlin laughed. "Karen loves teaching boys and just tolerates us men. Education is her first love and always will be. The lady will be teaching boys when she's ninety, but we'll all love her. Even you old, stale, married boys have got a warm spot in your heart for her.''

"I ain't married!" Breene bellowed.

"Oh, I forgot. You're just stale.''

The tussle that ensued was all in fun, but Jory Breene was wicked with his fists. If Brownlin hadn't been twice his size and quick on his feet, Jory would have beat him to a pulp, though all in fun.

Kyle took note of Jory Breene's love of fighting and his ability. He stayed and watched the scuffle draw to an end, with each man laughing as he staggered in the dirt, trying to stand upright. Kyle helped both men back on their feet now that the dust had settled.

The trio entered the town with Jory and Brownlin slapping the dust off their clothes. The men grinned and shook hands, then parted and went their separate ways. Kyle moseyed on down to the chair where he had sat the night before, watching the town. He was seated there when Bolden and his crew rode back into town from the cemetery. Bolden stopped his horse in the middle of the street and began to stare at Kyle. His riders did the same.

"Who are you, Rivers?" Bolden asked.

"Nobody."

"The devil you ain't!"

Bolden spurred his horse almost angrily and made the beast jump into stride. Once in motion, the group put their eyes ahead and ignored Kyle. A movement near Kyle's right side almost caused him to start as he looked up into the lawman's steady eyes.

"Bolden knows something about you."

Kyle shrugged. "Whatever it is is news to me."

The lawman reached to the other side of Kyle and grabbed a chair. He set the chair against the wall on Kyle's right and sat down on it. Kyle got to his feet.

"Sit down, Rivers," the lawman growled.

He was not a man to push, but Kyle made no move to sit. Instead, he saw a support post for the porch and leaned back against it.

"You're watching this town like a hawk," the lawman said. "Who are you looking for?"

Kyle kept mute. His look told the lawman he had no intention of answering. The lawman tried again.

"I might know him and save you a lot of looking."

Kyle looked down at his boots.

"You could have kept peace with me, Mr. Rivers. Now you're about to have a little trouble. Get on about your business. By the way, if you're still here packing that gun on your hip tomorrow, I'll relieve you of it until you leave."

Kyle choked back a retort that demanded to loose itself: *You'll try!* He stiffly walked away, barely keeping his temper.

Karen McLaughlin smiled at the lawman as she came down the walk after attending the funeral, and he offered her the chair beside him that Kyle had vacated. She sat down and turned dancing brown eyes on him.

"Julian Roman, how is your world today?"

"Slightly threatened," he said with a low laugh.

"By whom?"

"Your friend Mr. Rivers."

Karen turned and watched Kyle enter the general store. Then she turned questioning eyes on Julian. "He threatened you?"

"No, no, nothing like that. I asked him a few questions and he just clammed up. The kind of hate he has for the law is the kind that gives lawmen nightmares."

"I can hardly believe it. What in the world did you ask him? He's usually agreeable, and he gets along with everybody else." She looked down into her lap, then back at Julian. "Well, he didn't with Johnny, but that was different."

"And if I don't walk real careful, Johnny and I will be lying side by side." Julian looked down the street. "Has he told you what he's doing here?"

"He said he was looking for someone. Maybe two people, because first he asked about a name, and then he wanted to know if I knew of a local man who was blond and had a scar across his face."

Julian straightened and looked sharply at her. "What'd you tell him?"

"No, of course. I know of no such man."

"No, I guess you wouldn't. That was before you came." He was lost in thought for a few moments. "What name did he ask about?"

"No name that fits here—Jeb Grosse."

Julian set his jaw and stared into the vastness of the bluffs beyond town. When he looked back at her, his tense manner relaxed into a smile, and then he stood up.

"You're right, no such person or persons here. Thanks for the information. And don't tell Mr. Rivers about this chat. I guarantee you he'll come uncorked.

He refused to give me the very information you just gave me.''

"Then you shouldn't have pressed me about it, Julian,'' she said sternly, and visibly upset. "I prefer to stay out of other people's business, but it seems I'm guilty of letting my tongue wag in what I thought was a casual chat with you. Are you and Mr. Rivers going to have trouble because of what I've told you?''

"No, not because of that. The trouble was already in the making last night, and anything you told me today has helped to avoid more trouble. You have caused nothing.''

"I can't promise not to tell him that I told you. If I've wronged him, I reserve the right to be able to square myself with him.''

Julian shrugged. "That's your choice. No harm will be done either way, but you might cause a temper flare, and you'd better stay a long way back when it happens, or you'll get burned in the heat of it.''

Julian tipped his hat and moved on down the walk. Karen gazed after him a moment, then clenched her hands. "I hate being a busybody!'' she whispered angrily, and then hurried toward the livery barn.

Danny Brown sat on the edge of the riverbank, letting his feet hang over the edge nearly six feet from the water. The fingers on his small hands gently moved in the grass. A large tear rolled down his freckled cheek. Danny wiped his mouth with the back of his sleeve and fought a knot that tangled in his throat. He struggled inwardly, trying to handle his loss, but his nine years of life couldn't handle the hardness, and he turned and rolled belly down on the grass and sobbed against the earth. "Aw, dog," he cried quietly. "Aw, dog...."

The lonely Saturday wound down to evening, and as the sun set, Danny gathered himself up and trudged toward Widow Brown's small homestead on the river. She was never cruel to him, but she was old, too old to have a child forced upon her to raise. She was of the old school that worked children hard for their keep, but Danny ate well and was warm in winter, and sometimes she held him just because a child will not thrive without some love. She also knew that very soon he would be on his own, because her days were not long. She didn't want him missing her in addition to coping with the hard world he already had to face alone. In a way, her coldness toward him was a kindness.

Danny came up the path to the rear of the cabin. He swallowed hard and stared at the hair-matted rug near the door, where his dog used to lie. Danny slowly got to his knees and rolled up the rug. He stuffed it behind the half-empty wood box that it was his job to keep full. The door opened and the widow studied him in the twilight.

"The box will be all right until morning," she said sternly, but her eyes didn't back up her voice. Suddenly she motioned him to her, and Danny came slowly, dragging his feet. She put her feeble hands around him and pulled him against her apron. "Danny, all these hard times will make you strong. God will give you something better someday." She tightened her grip, then released him.

Danny stared at the folds of her apron for a moment. Then his eyes traveled up to her face. His smile told her thanks for the hug. He sobered and turned toward the wood box.

"I feel better when my work's done," he said. "Mrs. Brown, I'm all cried out. Am I grown up now because I can't cry no more?" He looked up at her.

"A sign of being grown is not making *other* people cry. It's not when *you* can't cry. Fill the wood box if it makes you feel better. Then come in and eat. By the way, Mr. Schweeney said he's got a pup for you."

"No, Mrs. Brown," he said quickly, and hurried away to where the ax lay in a stump.

Danny chopped more wood than the wood box would hold. The moon gave some light, and he worked on, burying his hurt in labor. Exhausted, he laid the ax aside and spent some time quietly sorting the chunks from the kindling. Suddenly a shot rang out from within the cabin. Danny froze with his small arms full of kindling. Then he let the load tumble to the ground as he ran to the back door and pulled it open.

The Widow Brown sat slumped in a chair at the table, her head on her arms. Danny swallowed hard and advanced into the kitchen on hesitant legs. He felt the wind blow through the cabin, and saw the front door swinging on its hinges. Vaguely, far out in the night, he heard a horse swiftly making its way across the rocks at the river crossing near the cabin. A trembling whimper escaped from his lips when he saw blood on the floor beneath her chair.

"Mrs. Brown?" he squeaked shakily.

She slowly opened her eyes and whispered his name.

"I'm here, Mrs. Brown," he answered in a broken voice.

"It's hard to tell you, Danny. Your mother. . . ."

Her eyes seemed to glaze, but they stayed open, staring at nothing. Danny stared and stared, then a tremble nearly shook him off his feet. Suddenly, there seemed to be things lurking everywhere in the cabin, things that were searching for him and whispering of death. He backed toward the door, spooked, and jumped at nothing. Next, with a stifled cry in his throat, he turned and ran from the cabin into the moonlight that guided his pounding feet through the dark, thick cedars.

Chapter Three

I N the gray dawn hours, Kyle made his way down the hallway toward the kitchen. He saw that the woman cooking was not Karen, so he bypassed it and turned into the dining room. He eased down into a chair in the dimness and studied the long length of the empty table that in an hour would be loaded with food. His mind toyed with Bolden's words when he had stopped in the street yesterday. The rancher's remark about his being "somebody" sparked his curiosity. Why was he a threat to Bolden? Shooting Johnny was a thing that Bolden could either avenge or drop. It was his choice, and Kyle should pose no threat to the man.

His mind drifted to the vendetta that had brought him to this town. He felt that the man he was looking for was not in Cedar Point, but, as yet, he had not made the rounds, asking for the man by name. He intended to do that today, and if the trail turned up totally cold, he'd move on to the next town.

The scent he followed had not been warm for many years. He searched for the man by sight first. Then, when it became evident he would come up empty-handed, he pried with questions. In this way, if the quarry were near, he would not be warned away before Kyle got a chance at him, and his questions would occasionally jolt an old memory that would give him another lead.

An outer door opened and closed, and then Kyle saw Karen step into the kitchen. She greeted the other woman, then turned and ambled into the dining room. It took her a moment to become aware of Kyle's presence at the large table. She smiled briefly and walked to a chair on the opposite side and sat down.

"Do you cook on Sunday too?" Kyle inquired.

"No."

"Then what brings the teacher into town?"

"You do, Mr. Rivers."

"I don't take well to lectures, Miss McLaughlin, if that's what you had in mind."

She shook her head and looked down at her lap for a moment. "Mr. Rivers, I am the one who must take the lecture. I did you an injustice yesterday and it troubled my sleep. I made up my mind to see you first thing this morning."

"First?"

"On Sunday I drive the buggy out to Widow

Brown's and pick her up so she can attend Sunday services here in town."

"And what is this injustice, Miss McLaughlin?"

"I told Julian who you were looking for."

"Julian?"

"The sheriff."

Kyle studied her with amusement on his face. She watched him shyly, then chanced her habitual quick grin.

"You're not mad?"

"Am I supposed to be?"

"Well, Julian thought you would be if you found out I'd told him. I didn't mean to talk behind your back."

Kyle gave a soft laugh. "It doesn't matter that he knows. I didn't tell him for the simple reason that he asked me. When the law questions a man, it's best to forget how to talk."

"I profoundly disagree with you on that point," she said firmly. "The law is a fair and just necessity."

His eyes narrowed, and the thing in them that seemed to make him dangerous fairly glowed like hot steel.

"Do you know of any other institution or agency in this country that can take your life and do with it as it dang well pleases without any more reason than the fact that some son of a—"

"*Mr. Rivers!*"

He went on: "*Someone* pointed an accusing finger at you!"

He jumped to his feet and crammed the chair up to the empty table with a loud crack. Then he leaned on the back of it and, swaying toward her almost threateningly, he said, "Your lawman will flirt with death this morning when he tries to take this gun off my hip!"

He turned and hurried from the dining room. Karen heard the outer door slam hard, and then the deep quiet in the dim and spacious room intensified to the point where she could not control a shudder. So that was the hate that gave lawmen nightmares. Karen could suddenly understand the danger that Julian had hinted at.

She went into the empty hallway. She had never before encountered the kind of danger like that lurking inside Kyle Rivers. It caused her a tingle of fright, but the feeling left as soon as she stepped into the warm morning sun. She mounted the seat of the buggy and reined the horse toward Widow Brown's cabin.

The blazing sun crept up the morning sky as Julian Roman carefully walked the boardwalks of his town. His worry was Kyle Rivers. He had made an ultimatum that he would stand by, merely because Kyle had blatantly defied him. Julian would ride it through, knowing full well that if Kyle showed himself this morning with the gun on his hip, a gunfight would ensue.

That worried Julian, not because he didn't have skill with a gun, but because Kyle had the advantage of age. Kyle's younger reflexes had to be better, and guns were all a game of reflex and accuracy. Julian tensely watched every doorway and opening between buildings. He knew that Kyle would show himself at his own chosen time.

It was near nine o'clock when Julian chanced by the livery barn. He strolled to the large opening and stood there, waiting for his eyes to adjust to the darkness within, when he became aware of Kyle leaning against a supporting timber. Julian cursed himself for his carelessness. Kyle had the advantage, because he himself was silhouetted against the sunlit street.

"I'm packing an iron," Kyle taunted softly.

"Are you sure it's worth it, Rivers?"

"As I see it, you didn't leave me much choice."

"You could have left town."

"Sure. Run, crawl, or fight—thanks, but I'll choose the one I can sleep with."

"You know that even if you win this, you lose," Julian said, killing time in an effort to get a clearer outline of Kyle's superior position.

"Somehow, you're not finding the right words to save your hide or mine, so let's get on with it," Kyle retorted in a smoldering tone.

"Julian! Julian!"

A carelessly driven buggy swayed dangerously, almost upsetting, as it made a jingling and clattering slide around the corner at the general store. Julian kept his hands high above his weapon and backed into the street. Karen McLaughlin charged her lathered buggy horse straight into the sheriff, causing him to jump aside as he leaped and grabbed the bridle on the heaving horse. The horse dragged him a few yards before coming to a stop.

"Julian!" Karen cried, tumbling out of the buggy into the dirt. She scrambled to her feet and plunged into his arms as he reached down to help her up. She cried out, "Mrs. Brown! Somebody murdered Mrs. Brown!"

Karen collapsed against him, out of breath and shaking. He grabbed her by the shoulders and studied her.

"Get hold of yourself! You're all mixed up, so calm down and get your head cleared out. Now tell me very slowly—what did you see?"

She shook clear of his grip, took a deep breath and then several more. In a totally calm and controlled voice, she leaned a tear-streaked face close to his as she answered.

"I saw Mrs. Brown slumped in the chair in her kitchen. She didn't move when I called out to her, so I went in and touched her shoulder. She was ice-cold and her skin was blue, and there was dried blood on the floor beneath her chair. And," she added angrily, "I assume that I have enough common sense to make the deduction that she was dead!"

Karen seemed to wilt as she finished, and she spun away from him. As Kyle walked out of the barn, she ran right into his arms. She glanced up rigidly for a moment, then reached around and clasped her arms behind his back.

"Please, take me where it's quiet," she whispered to him.

"Just a minute," Julian ordered. "Karen, you said she was murdered. How do you—"

"Why don't you just go look, lawman?" Kyle snapped.

Julian was taken aback for a few moments, but then he cleared his throat. "Excuse me," he said. "Maybe my brain ain't always as all-fired clear as I think it is." He allowed Kyle to see him study the grip he had on Karen. Then his eyes traveled down to the gun on Kyle's thigh. "We'll continue our earlier conversation at a later date, Rivers."

Julian yelled for a posse as he ran past Kyle and Karen and into the livery barn. He kept his horse saddled during the day, and within seconds he came out into the sunshine, mounted and gaining speed.

"Meet me at Brown's cabin!" he roared at the men gathering.

Julian rounded the corner at the general store and disappeared from their sight. One by one and in groups, townsmen rode out in haste, leaving the streets of Cedar Point in an uproar of dust.

Kyle kept a supportive arm around Karen and gently guided her into the coolness of the livery barn. She swayed against him as they walked. He indicated the ladder to the loft and they climbed up there. It was dark and cool, but most of all it was quiet.

They sank down against the hay. Karen rested in his

arms with her head against his shoulder. The scene of Mrs. Brown would not leave her mind, and she lingered long in his arms. When she finally raised her head, she had totally recovered her composure.

"I'm a little embarrassed now that I've calmed down. Heavens, Mr. Rivers, you're a total stranger. Thank you for not making me feel foolish. Julian really irritated me so, treating me like a kindergarten child, and I really did need an arm to lean on. I've heard women say they just needed someone to hold them, and it never quite made sense, but I understand it now."

"I didn't mind, Miss McLaughlin." His voice rumbled in a low, pleasing way.

She smiled at him, and her eyes twinkled slightly. He took notice of her dirt-stained face, but made no comment. It was the person he was seeing, not the features. Karen sobered and searched his gray eyes.

"I don't think that I minded, either," she whispered, suddenly drawn to the man who cradled her in his arms.

"Teacher, you're gonna get an answer to that," he murmured as his eyes traveled over her face, which was only inches from his.

"You're going to kiss me, aren't you?" she whispered dazedly, making the question a statement as the meaning of his words sank in. "Don't kiss me," she said, her voice muffled with a kind of tremble.

"Yes," he said softly.

Kyle barely touched his lips on hers, and lingered

there for a moment, brushing a gentleness against her lips that caused her to raise her hand to his jaw. Karen's breath caught in her throat as his hand slipped up her neck to the base of her hairline. Then his lips pressed firmer in a yearning caress.

Kyle felt her begin to struggle with him, and quickly turned his face aside, pressing her head into the hollow of his shoulder. His breathing was heavy and deep for a bit, then it leveled out and he softly laid his cheek against her hair.

"Don't be afraid of me," he said. "I'm sorry. It's been a long time. I'd almost forgotten how sweet it is."

He firmly pushed her away and got to his feet, pulling her up with him. A casual grin crossed his lips as his eyes flicked down over her clothing. He reached and slowly picked hay from her clothes, all the while grinning just a little.

"Thank you," she said, suddenly picking at herself. "I'd be terribly embarrassed to have walked out into the street with hay sticking to me after the whole town saw me go into the barn with you."

She quickly took a tally of him and immediately plucked at a few stems and leaves. He reached out and turned her around and set about picking off the hay that clung to her back. He noticed the tinge of blush on her cheeks and neck.

"You embarrass easily," he drawled.

"I'm sorry. I don't mean to."

"Oh, it's not a bad thing, Miss McLaughlin. No, not offensive in the least."

Kyle finished and turned her back around. He sobered and looked deeply into her eyes. He liked Karen McLaughlin a lot . . . a lot more like than a man engaged in a deadly game could allow himself. Sweet emotion had no place to rest inside him.

"Let's go down," he snapped coldly.

Karen fairly jumped at the instant change of mood. She peered curiously at him, but he spun round and descended to the stable floor below. When she reached the bottom also, he was going over his black horse with his hands. His cool manner hinged on rudeness. She watched him for a moment, waiting for him to look at her. But he didn't.

"You much resemble a door, Mr. Rivers," she said.

"How's that?"

"You slam shut depending upon the direction of the wind."

He straightened and gave her an indifferent look, but her look was akin to the blistering kind. He felt its heat long after she had left him there in the barn, alone, with his horse for company.

Julian Roman dismounted near the open door of the cabin. He had ridden in in a manner that didn't disturb the tracks leading from the door. The door was ajar and he could see through the house to the kitchen. He set his jaw as he stepped up on the porch. Then he stepped back as his eyes perceived an object on the ground. He reached down and picked up the .45 caliber shell, and then saw several more scattered under the porch. He got to his knees and looked under, then slowly backed away from the porch, intent on the grass at his feet. He bent and picked up another and another. It looked as if a whole handful had fallen to the ground.

Julian searched a moment longer, then entered the cabin. A short while later he reappeared at the open doorway. The stout lawman brushed at his eyes and blinked. Then he stared off into the trees with a knot in his chest and his lips pulled tight.

Several men rode toward him and he saw more coming up behind. He took a deep breath, brushed his eyes again, and then turned and faced the approaching riders. He motioned them away from the path in front of the cabin. Henry Tritch was the lead rider, followed by Reuben Sparks and Jory Breene.

"Go back to town and get your wagon, Rube. She's dead," Julian said gruffly.

The undertaker scowled, and his bony frame trembled for a moment. "What happened?"

"I haven't got that figured yet, but it was murder. The widow was shot in the back!"

Many more men had joined them by now, and Julian's words brought an angry roar from the group. Reuben Sparks looked sick as he slipped weakly into the rocker on the porch. He put his face in his hands. Rube and Mrs. Brown had never missed a single fall dance in fifteen years. This was going to be a hard one for the undertaker.

"Can you handle this?" Julian asked, squeezing Reuben's skinny shoulder.

"I wouldn't let anybody else do it. Give me a minute."

Julian ordered the group not to make a lot of tracks around the place, and when they did see tracks, to come and get him. He sent men down toward the river and into the cedar grove behind the house. He motioned to Jory and Tritch to come inside the cabin.

"We've got a big problem."

Jory said, "There isn't a man in this community that could be a suspect, and there ain't one cussed reason anybody would do such a thing to an old lady, and—Kripes! Where's Danny Brown? He had to have seen this, for heaven's sake!"

"That's the big problem. The kid was as shy and spooky as a fox pup before, and after this I'll bet he won't come to any of us. Winter is around the corner, and if we don't locate Danny real soon, we'll be finding what's left of him when the spring snow melts."

Tritch said, "When the snow falls, we could track him better."

"Yeah, but don't you reckon that might be too late? It only takes one cold night." Julian looked at Breene and raised his brows. "Got any suggestions?"

"No, except to say that the kid might also be in danger. What if he saw what happened here and somebody has to find him to shut him up?'' Breene chewed his lip for a minute, and scowled deeper and deeper. When he looked up at Julian and Tritch, a fire blazed in his eyes.

"What?'' Julian whispered.

"It's them blasted cowboys! They're getting even for Rivers' shooting their foreman for shooting the kid's dog! That's what this is all about!'' Breene bellowed.

"Just hold it right there!'' Julian rasped hoarsely, and he grabbed Breene by the collar. "This wasn't done by no cowboy, no farmer, no Indian, no trapper, mule skinner, or town drunk! This was done by a man, Breene. A single, individual, cowardly man! Don't you put fuel on a smoldering range war with an accusation like that!''

Breene drew back a doubled fist, but Julian grabbed it in midswing. Breene shook loose and drew back his fist again.

"Hit me and I'll put you behind bars!'' Julian promised coldly. He shook a fist at Breene and said, "It's over. Keep your trap shut about your lamebrain ideas, and let's find Danny Brown and the man that did this.''

Kyle sat on the boardwalk with his chair inclined against the wall. Sunday services weren't going well for the preacher, and Kyle grinned in amusement off and on as the man gathered up groups of whispering townspeople and ushered them into the church for the sermon. Soon they would come trailing out one by one, waiting and wondering what the sheriff would find at Mrs. Brown's.

Talk buzzed, and the preacher came out and repeated his actions several times, but to no avail. Finally he stepped up in an empty wagon box and began preaching from a four-wheeled pulpit attached to a sleeping team of sorrels. The man's voice carried down the street with extreme clarity, and Kyle got the full impact of the fire-and-brimstone tongue-lashing that was obviously striking fear in the hearts of the congregation. It didn't set well with Kyle that the preacher seemed to take such joy in terrorizing his flock. The man reminded Kyle of a bear on the rampage, and he longed to give him a taste of his own medicine.

Suddenly an image of the bearskin on the wall of the general store flashed in his mind, and with a laugh, he jumped up and rushed over to the store to borrow it, determined to show the preacher what it felt like to be face-to-face with a bear.

Only Mrs. Tritch, who didn't speak much English, was inside the store. Kyle made some gestures that he thought would make her understand he was only borrowing the bearskin, but before he was out the door, she had grabbed a broom and was yelling at him in German. He tried to hinder her pursuit by tying the door latch to a nearby hitching post. After all, he intended to come right back.

He threw the bearskin over himself and crept up to

where the preacher could see him but not the congregation. He didn't want to scare all those good folks.
The problem was, he'd forgotten about the horses.
While he was gone, one of the boys had sneaked over
and untied them, probably hoping they'd take the
preacher away. Now, as Kyle lurched forward and
grunted, the sorrels responded by sinking back, legs
stiff, nostrils flaring, and eyes bulging.

At that first lurch of the wagon, the preacher flipped
over the single seat behind him and landed legs up,
with his head on the floor. Then the team leaped into
the air, neck to neck, jerking the front wheels of the
wagon up with them. As the preacher struggled to right
himself, he took another dive and landed with only his
gripping fingernails visible to the crowd. The team,
wagon, and preacher took off, rounding the corner at
the general store in a spewing cloud of dust.

Kyle hadn't intended to spook the horses, but they
were gentle, well-trained animals, and he was sure that
they would soon calm down and that their fire-and-
brimstone cargo would be safe. He hurried off to return
the borrowed bearskin to its rightful place on the wall,
but Mrs. Tritch was waiting for him outside the store,
and she began hitting him on the head with her broom.
He figured it would be a lot safer just to drop the hide
and take off.

As the sun skipped past the noonday sky, Reuben
Sparks returned to town, but he soon left again, driving

a team and buckboard. The sheriff returned shortly after that, but after the frantic gesturing and shouting of half a dozen townspeople, he left again at a high lope. Kyle attempted to question several people about Jeb Grosse, but all anyone would discuss was the murder of Mrs. Brown. He saw Karen several times, but she stayed away from him.

Around three o'clock the sheriff returned with another man and the preacher, who had one arm bandaged. Kyle chose to bow out as that situation headed his way, and he ducked into the saloon and let them pass. When he stepped back on the boardwalk, he saw the stableman headed toward the barn, and a little fire jumped into Kyle's eyes. He quickly followed the man into the livery.

Once inside the barn, the fellow set to work removing manure from the tie stalls into a wagon. Kyle walked up and leaned against a beam and glared at the man. The man turned with a start and cried, "Criminy! Say something. You scared me to death."

"I got a bone to pick with you," Kyle growled.

"Hey, I ain't got no fight with a gunfighter. I ain't fighting, whatever it is."

"I don't cotton to anybody riding my horse when I leave him in the care of a livery."

"Sir, I've never ridden a horse that was left in my barn, I swear . . . I swear," he said, sweating a bit in nervousness.

"This morning around ten o'clock I rubbed my horse

down and there was dried sweat all over him. He was rode hard last night.''

''Mister, I swear—if that horse was ridden, I didn't know anything about it!''

Kyle studied the man a few moments, then walked away. He was satisfied that the man didn't know about it. But that didn't change the fact that the horse had had a night ride. He decided to start keeping an eye on the barn at night until he left Cedar Point. It was his habit to leave the bulk of his supplies in his saddlebags on his saddle, but now he'd take the precaution of keeping the bags in the boardinghouse.

He stepped out of the livery and hesitated when he saw the lawman chatting out in front of the general store with Mrs. Tritch. It looked like a good time to saddle up and scout out the nearby country and thus avoid the lawman and Mrs. Tritch.

An hour after sunset Kyle rode back into Cedar Point. He put up his horse and went to the boardinghouse. He'd missed supper, but that was fine as long as he'd also missed Mrs. Tritch's accusing finger. He made his way to the bunk room, and as he slid out of his clothes and tucked the .45 under his pillow, he noticed that several men already slept while a few others lounged on their beds, reading and talking.

He sighed tiredly, glad that no harm had come of his deviltry. For the life of him, he didn't know what had made him do it. He lay awake for a long time, staring up into the rafters. When he heard the door open, he thought it was one of the boarders. When he heard no one advance farther than the foot of his bed, he pulled his gaze from the ceiling and looked into the faces of Henry Tritch, the preacher, Mrs. Tritch, and Rolf Schweeney. Julian Roman planted a stern eye on him from a position too close to allow Kyle time to reach under his pillow for the .45 Colt.

"It was him!" Mrs. Tritch cried in a heavy accent, stretching an arm and accusing finger directly at Kyle.

"Yes," the preacher said, nodding and babying his wrapped-up arm, "that's the man I saw beside the church."

"Mr. Rivers," Rolf Schweeney thundered angrily, "did you frighten my horses at the church today?"

Kyle glanced at Julian and held his tongue. Julian pulled his weapon and stepped in close to Kyle's bedside. He rammed the bore into Kyle's chest, then reached under the pillow and pulled Kyle's .45 into view. He dropped the revolver into the holster hanging on the bedpost, then slung the whole business over his shoulder.

"Mr. Rivers," he purred, "you're under arrest."

Chapter Four

KYLE made no move to get out of bed. He knew that he needed to get his temper under control. As it was, if he moved, he'd do something violently stupid and undoubtedly end up shot for his mistake.

"Get up, Rivers," Julian barked.

Kyle glanced at Mrs. Tritch, then at Henry. "Send your wife out. I'm dressed like Adam and Eve."

Tritch quickly spoke to his wife. She blushed and left the room.

"Up, Rivers," Julian ordered again.

Kyle threw back the covers so quickly that Julian crouched and flinched with his thumb playing on the hammer of his gun. Kyle pulled on his pants, eyeing the lawman contemptuously. They looked like two tomcats squaring off. If they had had the ability to lay back their ears and bare their fangs, they probably would have done so. Kyle stood up after pulling on his boots, and turned his back on Julian.

"Henry, Rolf," Julian ordered, "put a gun on him."

As soon as the men had their guns leveled at Kyle, Julian holstered his own and reached for the handcuffs on his belt. The first cuff came shut on Kyle's wrist with a snap. Then, when Julian grasped Kyle's other wrist to pull it behind him and secure the handcuffs, he saw the ragged scars that were usually hidden from view by his shirtsleeves. Julian slowly closed the iron into the catch, studying the marks around Kyle's wrists. He stepped around his prisoner and looked him in the face. The lawman's eyes held curiosity and a wave of something Kyle couldn't read.

Julian turned toward the other men and said. "Thanks. I can handle it from here."

He continued to study Kyle for some time after the two others had left. Choosing not to look directly back, Kyle stared across the room at nothing.

"Been in prison, haven't you, Rivers?" Julian asked softly, so that his question wouldn't be overheard by the others.

Still silent, Kyle continued to stare across the room.

"Your eyes follow prison customs. You never look a guard in the eye. He might see your hate."

Kyle didn't react to anything Julian said.

"A man doesn't get the scars you carry from correction. Those are signs of abuse to a man who can't fight back."

Kyle's eyes shifted slightly, then suddenly swung around and settled on Julian. He didn't speak. Abruptly his eyes traveled back across the room.

Julian snorted with a shrug, "Well, at least that's something, little as it is. Rivers, you're under arrest for theft, disturbing the peace, and causing injury to people and property. Head for the jail."

Kyle moved out sharply, and Julian had to move fast to keep up with him. Julian opened the door that led into the cell room at the back of his office. He sent Kyle through with a gentle shove, then locked him in one of the barred enclosures.

After the cuffs were removed, Kyle walked to the far side of the cell and gripped the bars on the window so tightly that, even in the lantern light, Julian could see the white in his knuckles. At the cell-room door, he looked back at Kyle. The man was trembling, and it wasn't the tremble of fear but of rage. Julian closed the door, tossed the gun belt from off his shoulder onto the desk, and then eased himself down into the chair.

He sat thoughtfully for a minute. Then he pulled a .45 shell from his pocket and studied it. Next, he reached over to Kyle's gun belt, pulled a shell loose, and rolled it in his fingers beside the one he had picked up at the door to Mrs. Brown's cabin. Suddenly Julian straightened up and put both hands under the lantern light on the desk. He rolled the shells again, then stared at the one he'd pulled from Kyle's belt. Both leads had come from the same loading die!

When a knock sounded at the door, Julian pocketed the shells and called out. The livery man stepped quickly inside and scrambled to a chair in front of Julian's desk. He leaned forward with a frightened look in his eyes.

"Sheriff, I got trouble," he whispered.

"What kind of trouble?"

"That gunfighter . . . Rivers. Well, he come down to the barn this afternoon and chewed the heck out of me for riding his horse last night. I never done it, Sheriff, and that gunman is gonna kill me if it happens again. Somebody's sneaking in at night and taking a ride, and it's gonna get me killed!"

Julian frowned. He leaned forward and peered into the man's face.

"Did you know the horse was ridden before Rivers jumped you about it?"

"No. He's the one that told me. I'd never have known if he hadn't said something."

"Thanks. Don't mention this to anyone else. I'll see that Rivers doesn't go after you for it."

"Thank you, Julian. He scares me somethin' awful."

After the man left, Julian again took the shells from his pocket and studied them. What had just come to light made him ponder thoughtfully for a long time. He watched the smoke rings from his pipe drift upward and make a gray fog on the ceiling.

Julian roused himself near midnight and walked

softly to the cell-room door. He looked in, as he'd done several times during the evening. Kyle still stood where he had since he'd entered the cell—in front of the window, hands gripped tightly around the bars. Julian opened the door and walked inside the cell room. He carried a chair in one hand and placed it across from Kyle's cell. Julian sat down, watching him.

"What'd you do to pull time, Rivers?" He didn't expect an answer from the man. He sat quietly for a while, then took a puff on his pipe and threw Kyle a low blow:

"I'm charging you with the murder of Widow Brown."

That brought Kyle around like a snarling cougar. He crossed the cell in three strides and grasped the bars in front of Julian.

"For *what?*" he yelled. "Because I played a stupid prank? And because you got the cursed law backing you up, you're gonna charge me with *murder?*" Angrily, he yanked the bars that held him prisoner, but though they shuddered, he could no more damage them than a leaf could fell a stout oak. "Aw, what's the use!" Kyle forced the words out through his teeth along with a groan of frustration. He pivoted and walked to the window again and took up his watch.

"You and I have some things to discuss, Rivers. You keep up the way you're doing, and you'll force me to play that card. It's your choice. Talk to me or hang yourself."

Julian picked up the chair and went toward the door. He glanced back at Kyle.

"Not all the law is bad, the same as every man that walks in and out of a prison ain't bad. You're too old for me to have to be explaining that to you."

Kyle and Julian locked eyes. Then Julian stepped through to the office and closed the door. Kyle stayed by the window for some time after that. His legs began to ache, so he shifted his weight and leaned to one side.

A hissing tick whipped lead between the window bars and the report of a gun exploded from beyond in the darkness. The lead hit the iron cell door and ricocheted crazily. It sent Kyle scrambling flat onto the floor. The bullet was silenced as it buried itself in a wooden bench near the door to the cell room.

Julian burst through the door, gun in hand. He located Kyle on the floor. "Are you hit?"

Kyle shook his head and Julian disappeared back through the door. A moment later Kyle heard him outside near the window. Then, much later, Julian again entered the cell room. He tossed Kyle a shirt through the bars.

"Put that on, the night's getting cold. Somebody wants you dead. Got any ideas?"

Kyle just glared at him.

Julian turned and swung open the office door to leave. "Well, if that's the way it's gonna continue between me and you, then you better keep your eyes open. Whoever it was will probably be back, and next time you'll have to scamper to dodge a closer shot.''

''You're gonna leave me locked in here where I can't get away from a bullet?'' Kyle demanded angrily.

''Loosen your jaw a little and I might move you to that cell around the corner from the window.''

Kyle clenched his jaw. He was a cornered target in the cell by the window and couldn't help but shoot a hungry look at the protection of the cell around the corner. The sheriff had him where he wanted. It would be pretty stupid to continue to refuse to talk to him.

''All right,'' he said quietly. ''What do you want to know?''

Julian dragged in a chair and sat down in front of Kyle's cell again. He filled his pipe and lit it, watching the puffs rise toward the ceiling. He set the stem in the corner of his mouth and folded his arms across his chest.

''How long was your stretch behind bars?''

''Six years.''

''What'd you do time for?''

''Something I didn't do,'' Kyle retorted bitterly.

''What is it you didn't do?''

''Rob a bank.''

''That's the usual denial.''

''I didn't do it,'' Kyle repeated quietly.

Julian studied the expression on his face and bored a shrewd eye into his. ''How'd they nail you to the wall then? There had to be enough evidence to get you sentenced.''

Kyle shrugged. ''A handful of shells and a borrowed horse. A witness saw my horse at the right place and right time. That's all the law wanted, not my side of it.''

Julian straightened slightly, and leaning forward on the chair, he scrutinized Kyle with an intensity that caused him to tense.

''Handful of shells?''

''Yeah, a handful. Not one accidentally dropped, not two fumbled from a cartridge belt, but a whole blessed handful, and nobody thought that strange at all. They didn't want to.'' A tremor of anger rampaged through Kyle, and he turned and paced back and forth to cool down. ''My side of the story didn't matter then, and telling you doesn't change the past, but, Sheriff, I'm not guilty of what you're laying on me.'' He grasped the bars in front of Julian. ''I've never been south of town, and I'm not the kind of man that would shoot an old woman in the back. You haven't got the evidence to pin that on me!''

''South of town?''

''Yeah, at the widow's cabin.''

''So, when were you there?'' Julian questioned carefully.

''I wasn't. I saw you ride that way this morning.''

''Your horse was out last night.''

Kyle stared at Julian.

''And I suppose you didn't ride him . . . gonna say

somebody else did, huh?'' Julian waited a few moments, then added, ''I found a handful of shells in the doorway to Mrs. Brown's cabin, and they're partners to the ones in your cartridge belt that's lying out on my desk.''

Kyle held his silence, but fiery light sprang into his eyes. When he spoke, his tone was bitter: ''Jeb Grosse is in this town.''

Julian studied him quietly. ''Is Jeb Grosse the man who pointed the finger at you, Rivers?''

''No, he's the man that dropped a whole handful of shells nine years ago!''

''How long have you been hunting Jeb?''

''Several years.''

''That's several years you wasted.''

''That's your opinion,'' Kyle answered.

''No, that's fact. You'll never kill Jeb Grosse,'' Julian said, watching Kyle, ''because Jeb Grosse died six years ago. And that makes it plain that he didn't plant any shells at the Widow Brown's.''

Coming to a decision, Julian got to his feet and went to the corner cell. He opened it and returned to Kyle's cell.

''Step back,'' he said, drawing his revolver.

Kyle obeyed as Julian put the keys to the lock and motioned him out and down to the other cell. As he locked the door behind Kyle, Julian said, ''Three things are fact, and one is that somebody wants you dead.''

"And the other two?"

"The shells I found at the widow's cabin are yours. The third thing is that you didn't kill Mrs. Brown."

Kyle's eyes opened in surprise. Julian removed the lantern from the wall hook, then nodded to Kyle as he closed the door to the cell room. "Good night. And by the way, Mrs. Brown lived west of town down by the river." He closed the door. Minutes later the lanterns in the outer room went out.

The morning sun was two hours old before the door opened to the cell room. The woman who cooked at the boardinghouse entered with a basket on her arm, and Julian came in behind her. She waited as the sheriff sorted through some keys. Then he nodded at Kyle.

"Step back."

The woman left the food without look or comment, and Julian relocked the cell door.

"Your judges will be in in about an hour. Better get your breakfast down." Julian gazed at the silent prisoner for a moment. Then he turned to leave.

"Morning, Sheriff," Kyle said quietly.

Julian stopped in his tracks and turned around. "So, you're gonna give it a chance. That surprises me, you being how you are."

"You surprised me last night, you being a man with access to the power of the law."

"You expected me to hang that murder on you with

a handful of shells and the fact that you've already had one trip to prison?''

''Why didn't you? You have the power. Nobody would have questioned you.''

''Because,'' Julian said, shooting a stern look at Kyle, ''I'm a lawman.''

Julian stepped through the doorway and left Kyle alone. Kyle found enough good breakfast in the basket to make him feel stuffed. He pondered the lawman as he ate, baffled by the fact that Julian Roman was a fair man. He had the power but he didn't abuse it. Two biscuits more than Kyle could eat lay staring at him from the basket, so he stuffed them into the pocket of his shirt to nibble on later.

Kyle's thoughts drifted to what Julian had said about his ''judges'' being there in an hour. He was trying to figure what was in the wind when the office door opened and a line of people came filing in—the preacher, Mr. and Mrs. Tritch, Rolf Schweeney, Jory Breene, and Brownlin. Julian brought up the rear.

They all lined up against the wall and put their full attention on Kyle. Julian announced that he would vote if there was a tie. Suddenly it became clear to Kyle: his victims were the witnesses, judge, and jury. He took a deep breath as the hearing got underway.

''What are the damages, Rolf?'' Julian began.

''My team of sorrels cannot be used to plow the fields until their shoulders heal. And my wagon . . . the buckboard is no more. I need a new wagon. The harnesses are torn and need mending.''

"And this damage was brought on because of what?"

"Well, the reverend said Mr. Rivers frightened the team. The sorrels ran between two cottonwood trees at a high speed. They barely fit between the tree trunks, and the wagon didn't."

"Reverend? Your damages, please," Julian said.

"Mine are slight compared to the others. Please, I have no anger against this man. My wrist is sprained but it will quickly heal. I feel, however, that Mr. Rivers needs some religious—"

"That's fine, Reverend. We'll get to that later. Henry Tritch?"

"Well, Julian, my wife has a hard time with the language, so I will speak for her. She tried very hard to keep Mr. Rivers from stealing the bear hide. When he came back to steal more, she beat him with the broom until he left."

"You got your bear hide back?" Julian inquired.

"Yes."

"Defend your actions, Rivers," Julian said gruffly.

"I can't," Kyle admitted.

"Did you spook the sorrel team?"

"Yes."

"Why?"

"I hadn't meant to. I didn't know they'd be untied. What I meant to do was spook the preacher."

Exclamations blurted from the lips of his accusers. Kyle set his jaw and shot a look at Julian. Kyle was a man who lived by his word. He would never lie, not even to save his life—and at the moment, it looked as if he might lose it.

"Why in the world did you want to do that?" Julian demanded.

Kyle saw that the questioning would gradually dig up the whole story, so he might as well tell it and get it over with. It was evident no one knew exactly what he had done.

"The reverend here was throwing brimstone all over the street from the bed of that wagon. He was acting like an angry bear, scaring the tarnation out of all those good folks. I thought it was time he got a bit of his own medicine." He sighed. "I didn't mean for him or for the horses to get hurt, or for the wagon to get busted." He paused, then burst out, "But—doggone it!—no man's got a right to scare a bunch of women and kids with horror stories like that!"

Jory Breene exploded in laughter, and Brownlin joined in. Then, like a group of schoolboys, the other men answered the call. The preacher and Mrs. Tritch stood somber and wide-eyed, shocked into silence by the men's amusement.

Julian was the first to recover. Wiping his eyes, he shook silently as he battled with mirth. Finally, he cleared his throat and hollered at the rest of them:

"Jory! Brownlin! And the rest of you! Straighten up! This is a court of law! Straighten up!"

Order was restored, and Julian addressed the

preacher: "What do you think would repay you for your inconvenience in this matter, Reverend?"

"I would merely like for Mr. Rivers to attend church, Sheriff."

"How many times?"

"Why, for the rest of his life."

"That's too long. Pick a number below five."

"Four?" the preacher ventured hesitantly.

"I sentence you to four Sundays in church, Mr. Rivers. You've already admitted guilt, so keep your mouth shut. Tritch? Name your penalty."

"We ain't hurt. No charge, Sheriff."

"Schweeney?"

"I want a new wagon. I want my harness mended. I want him to work in the field until he has paid for the loss of my horses."

"Mr. Rivers, I sentence you to three weeks' labor under Mr. Schweeney here." Julian turned to Jory and Brownlin. "Is this judgment and sentence agreeable with the court?"

"What if he don't do it?" Jory asked.

"If he doesn't show up for work, I'll jail him and take him out there at gunpoint. If he leaves the country, I'll put out a warrant for his arrest and add a reward on top of it."

"And if he don't go to church?"

"You two deputies will escort him."

Jory and Brownlin talked softly for a while, then both nodded. "Court agrees with the decision."

"Court adjourned."

As quickly as they had entered the room, the group left. Julian studied Kyle for a minute, then left also, but abruptly returned and unlocked the cell door. He swung open the iron and nodded.

"Come out front."

Kyle followed Julian to the office and stood beside the desk as Julian sat down. The lawman looked up at him.

"Well?" Julian inquired.

"Are you asking what I think of your justice?"

"Yep."

"It was fair."

Julian pulled open a large drawer on the desk and reached inside. He laid Kyle's gun belt and revolver on the desktop, then leaned back in his chair and studied Kyle.

"If you shirk your sentences, I'll do as I said." Julian saw Kyle glance down at the gun belt on the desk. "You keep the peace with me, and you can wear your gun. If and when I think you're a threat to this town, I'll take it from you. You're free to go. Don't bother the livery man again about your horse, and show up at Schweeney's farm tomorrow morning at sunup."

Kyle picked up the gun belt, buckled it around his hips, and then tied the leather thong above his knee. He looked long but not aggressively at Julian.

"Just try taking it from me, Julian," he whispered.

Then a half-grin crossed his lips. "But I won't give you a reason to try."

"I'd appreciate that. Rivers, somebody out there is trying to kill you. I'm not sure yet if that's linked to the murder or not, but I don't have to warn you to stay sharp." Julian's eyes became shrewd. "Do you have any idea who is after you?"

"Only Jeb Grosse."

"I told you, he's dead."

Kyle leaned toward Julian and searched his unyielding eyes. "Are you protecting Jeb?"

"My first impulse is to black your eyes for calling me a liar. My second is to tell you to go up to the cemetery. The grave is on the north side."

At the door, Kyle turned back and said, "Was the murdered woman the widow who took in little Danny Brown?"

"Yes."

"Where's the boy?"

"God only knows. I've had a search going since yesterday morning, but all we've turned up is tracks. Always one set. He never comes back over his same trail. I could use some help on that score, Rivers, so if you see him, try to get your hands on him."

"Because he might know something about the widow's murder that will help you?" Kyle asked baitingly.

Julian caught his tone, and quickly calculated what he was fishing for. "No," he said softly. "Get your hands on him because the little feller's a lost soul and he needs a warm shoulder and a place to sleep.''

''Lawman, if you ever need a gun on your side . . . .'' Kyle nodded and pulled the door shut. He stepped down onto the boardwalk but looked back at the door. Julian wasn't merely the law. He was a man. Kyle glanced up at the late-morning sun. Then he headed toward the cemetery.

Chapter Five

T HE graveyard was a quarter mile from the last building on the edge of town. Kyle walked intently, a frown on his face. Reuben Sparks was latching the black iron gate as Kyle came up. Noticing the curtained hearse wagon, Kyle looked questioningly at Rube.

"Widow Brown," the undertaker mumbled. "Lots of folks came. She was a good woman." He lifted the latch and let the gate swing for Kyle to enter the cemetery. "Close it when you leave." Rube quickly climbed to the seat of the wagon and clucked to the team.

Kyle meandered through the northern section of graves, reading each headstone before moving on to another. He was walking past fancy ironwork around several granite markers when his eyes settled on the large letters GROSSE FAMILY carved on a flat plate on the ironwork. He quickly read the names on the graves: *Amos and Clare, Nate, Will,* and *Elsie,* and there in front of his eyes, *Jeb Grosse.* Stunned, Kyle stared at the headstone.

Like the fatigue that follows a burning fever, an inner exhaustion caused Kyle to turn slowly and sit on the ground with his back against the iron fence. The date on the grave indicated that Jeb had been dead for four years when Kyle began to search for him.

As vividly as if it were now happening, Kyle envisioned Jeb's dancing eyes and triumphant smirk as he flashed a fistful of shells before Kyle's eyes as Kyle was removed from the courtroom in chains and under heavy guard. Kyle's fingers curled as he relived leaping toward Jeb but being clubbed to the floor by the guards. Six years of his life had been taken from him by the law, and several more had been wasted on nothing.

The sun rolled toward noon, and its hot rays warmed Kyle dizzily, making the nothingness more intense. The total lack of violence and lack of reward at the end of his vengeful pursuit drenched him with the awareness that, in the end, Jeb had managed to rob him of even more.

"And where is she, Jeb Grosse? You cost me more than the years!" he whispered.

With his head against the ironwork, Kyle gazed out across the cemetery. Not thirty feet away, a fresh mound of dirt seemed to leer back at him. Sitting down cross-legged against the mound, Danny Brown rubbed a dirty sleeve across his eyes and sniffled lightly. Kyle sat up with a snap. That quick movement caught Danny's attention, and he twisted his head and shot a look over his shoulder.

Kyle stared and Danny stared. Neither moved for several moments. Carefully, slowly, Kyle leaned back against the ironwork, searching his mind for words that would hold the frightened boy where he was. Danny held his ground, but Kyle saw that he was on the edge of flight.

Suddenly Kyle remembered the biscuits and took one from his shirt pocket. He took a bite and munched it slowly, all the while watching Danny. The boy watched him chew, then moistened his lips and swallowed, staring at the biscuit in Kyle's hand. Kyle reached in his pocket and withdrew the other biscuit. He extended his hand toward Danny, and though the boy looked hungrily at the food, he didn't make a move toward it.

Aware of the fear in the boy's eyes, Kyle kept the biscuit in view and slowly got to his feet. He took a few steps toward a flat-topped headstone and laid the biscuit there. Then he backed off and sat down again. He continued to nibble at the biscuit in his hand, his eyes on the boy.

Danny responded quickly. He got to his feet and went over to the biscuit. He grasped it and ate it ravenously. As soon as it disappeared, his eyes locked on what was left of the one in Kyle's hand. Kyle extended it, but this time he didn't get up. Danny shook his head and said, "No."

"If you want it, come and get it," Kyle said softly.

"No. You'll catch me and send me to one of those orphan places."

"Who told you that?"

"The boys at school. They said that when Mrs. Brown died, I'd have to go to one of them places 'cause I didn't have no kin. I ain't goin'."

"You don't have to go if you have a job and you go to school. Here, take this biscuit. I can't eat any more."

Danny shook his head. "No. You lay it on this here headstone." He backed away, watching Kyle carefully.

Kyle got up, placed the biscuit on the granite, then sat down again. He watched Danny pounce on the bit of food and wolf it down.

"You're alone now and you're just gonna have to grow up faster than the other boys. First you need a job. Then you need to go to school so you can show everybody you're taking proper care of yourself and you're willing to work. Orphan homes are for boys that can't take care of themselves."

Danny's eyes studied Kyle distrustfully. He shot a glance toward the seclusion of a clump of berry bushes near the edge of the cemetery, then gave Kyle a sideways look.

"Nobody would give me a job. I'm only nine years old."

"Well, it just so happens that I need somebody about that age. I've got a job a man wouldn't take, and the rest of the boys have got chores at home and can't do it. Tell you what, Danny. If you'll go to work for me, I'll pay your board and room at the boardinghouse. You can have all you want to eat every day and a warm bed to sleep in."

Danny's eyes widened with interest. Then he gave Kyle another distrustful look.

"What do I have to do?"

"I got myself in trouble by breaking up Mr. Schweeney's wagon. I have to work for him a couple of weeks, and that means my horse has to leave every morning and come back every night before and after the livery feeds. I'll need someone to feed him and unsaddle him at night, brush him, then get up early and feed him before I have to leave."

"If I do that, are you sure they won't make me go away?" Danny asked.

"They'll have to whip me to do it," Kyle said with the hint of a grin. "Of course, you'll have to go to school every day too. Otherwise, I can't hire you."

"I like school," he said, looking at the ground. "And I like Miss McLaughlin. I just didn't know what to do since . . ." His eyes strayed to the mound of fresh earth, then shot back at Kyle. "I'm big now, big enough to work, but Mrs. Brown always said a man had to think things out before he did things. So I reckon I better go think about it.''

Danny sprang into flight so quickly that Kyle started. But, continuing to sit, he watched Danny dive through the headstones toward the cemetery fence. The boy scaled the fence and leaped out of sight into the cover of the thicket.

Kyle got to his feet and looked thoughtfully toward the opening in the bush where Danny had disappeared. For a few long moments he continued to look. Then he turned his attention to Jeb Grosse's grave. Finally he shrugged and left.

About twenty minutes later, Kyle stood hesitantly in front of Julian's office. Finally he turned the latch and walked in. Julian looked up from some paperwork and leaned back in his chair. A gentle smile crossed his lips as he nodded in approval.

''Back in here of your own accord?''

Kyle studied him silently, choosing his words carefully before he spoke. ''What happens to Danny Brown when you catch him?''

''Well, I'm not sure. If no one wants to take him in, I guess we have to contact the territory officials and have him sent to a home for boys.''

''What if he gets a job and takes care of himself and goes to school?''

''He's got to have a guardian. I just can't let a nine-year-old boy be on his own.''

"Why not?" Kyle snapped.

"Because of the law." As Julian saw a gleam of fire enter Kyle's eyes, he pursed his lips and took a minute to ponder what he'd just said. "Then again," he continued, a hint of light suddenly in his own eyes, "I'd say that maybe the law is flexible about boys nobody cares about."

"He's going to work for me and he'll be going to school. Will the law leave him alone?"

"Are you going to answer for him?"

"I won't need to. He'll answer for himself. Will you leave him alone?"

"It's apparent that you've talked to him."

Kyle nodded.

"Well, Rivers, I'll put it this way. I won't do anything about the boy as long as I see he eats, has a warm bed, goes to school, and somebody takes the time to see that he stays out of trouble. When a single one of those things goes unattended, the law will step in."

Kyle nodded slowly. "That's good enough."

He went back out on the street and made his way toward the livery barn. A little later he rode the black out of Cedar Point and reined him toward the farmers' school.

The early afternoon swirled small dust devils across the schoolyard as Kyle dismounted near the well and led his horse to a nearby tree. The only sound in the stillness of the cloudless day was Karen McLaughlin's clear voice. It rose and fell pleasingly on Kyle's ears.

He leaned against the tree in full view of the windows along one side of the structure and was able to see Karen's form silhouetted against a window on the far side. He waited for her to look out and discover his presence.

Inside, Karen turned from the blackboard and looked at Simeon Schweeney as she pointed to a shape she had drawn with the chalk.

"Which continent is that?"

"Acirfa," Simeon answered, stifling a smirk.

"Quite correct," Karen said, totally ruining Simeon's attempt to disrupt the class. She indicated to another student. "Willard, what kind of animals live here?"

"Snoil, arbez, and phantelas," he answered, then doubled up laughing.

Karen studied both boys coolly, without the least hint of a smile on her face. "Willard, you failed to turn the word 'elephant' around so the other pupils could understand you. Therefore, you will write the word one hundred times and turn it in with your homework in the morning. Simeon, I am just delighted that you know the continents backward and forward, so you will turn in, along with your regular homework, twenty drawings of all the continents. You will write the continents' names across the drawings, both forward and backward."

As Karen turned back toward the blackboard, her eyes swept the scene outside the window. After a quick breath, she looked again and turned to the class.

"I hope that there will never be a repetition of this. Next time, I will have a chat with your parents. Now I feel that there is the need for a recess. Simeon, Mr. Rivers is waiting outside. Please see what he wants."

Kyle watched the farmers' children come ripping out of the schoolhouse, wrestling and laughing. Simeon Schweeney came directly over to him.

"Miss McLaughlin is curious why you came," he said. Admiration glowed in his eyes as they stared at Kyle's gun. He looked up at Kyle and asked eagerly, "Would you teach me how to shoot fast?"

"No," Kyle said coolly. "And my business with Miss McLaughlin is not for a messenger."

Kyle walked around Simeon and made his way to the schoolhouse. He stepped inside and saw Karen sitting at her desk with her hands folded. He made his way across the room to the desk and looked down into her eyes.

"Well, Mr. Rivers, I see the door opens. Apparently the wind changed for a bit," she said icily.

"Maybe what swings the door is something you shouldn't question," Kyle said. He bent enough to put his hands on the desk and lean toward her.

"Mr. Rivers, I dislike your superior attitude, and I resent your taking advantage of me yesterday. I will not put up with you today."

"Well, maybe I'm not giving you any choice."

"You cannot intimidate me today, Mr. Rivers. This is my domain, and I won't put up with your bad manners and rude behavior!"

"Ma'am, I was once bossed by a woman and I didn't take it then and I won't now. Maybe the door swings shut to protect you from something. Maybe the door swings shut to protect me. Maybe you haven't been where I've been, and you sure as heck won't know where I've gone when I'm gone. So, don't try to cut a bloody hole in me with a sharp tongue, because you're wasting your time and mine!"

Karen looked away, nervously shuffling papers on the desk, and trying to control the color that heated her cheeks. She took a deep breath and said softly, "I didn't mean to start a war, Mr. Rivers."

Kyle straightened and turned his head toward the window. He looked outside long enough to get control of what had made him explode. When he looked back at her, there was no fight in his eyes.

"Well, you're right. I'm an obnoxious critter," he said, offering a faint smile. She smiled briefly, then turned her attention to the papers on her desk. "Miss McLaughlin, I came about Danny Brown."

Karen looked up quickly. "Have you seen him?" she asked with concern.

"Yes, and I talked to him. He wants to come to school, but he's afraid of an orphan home. I talked to Julian, and he's agreed to let the boy alone as long as he attends school and somebody keeps an eye on him. The reason I'm here is to ask you not to do anything different because of what's happened. He's a boy who's spooked, and it won't take many mistakes from grown-ups for him to skedaddle on to different pastures.''

"Mr. Rivers, you don't have to tell me about Danny. I am the one who spent months winning his trust enough to get him to come to school. The big battle was getting him to mix with the other children so he would come to school willingly. I had worried that I hadn't made enough progress, but now I know that I have, because he told you he wanted to come back to school." When she looked at him, he saw a dampness in her eyes that showed her deep feelings for Danny. "Thank you for telling me."

"He'll be coming back to school in the morning if things work out. Kinda watch the other boys. If one of the bigger ones gets to picking too hard on Danny, let me know. I won't have any of that. School is a good place to learn fairness."

"You like children," she said, nodding and smiling.

"You said that once before," he muttered.

"How is it that you haven't managed to have any of your own?"

Kyle flushed and looked out the window. "I should have had . . . but I was sent away. When I returned, she was gone," he finished bitterly. He looked back at Karen, and seconds ticked by. "I guess it was all for the best. We fought something awful."

"You're married?" she asked under her breath, quickly looking down.

"No, she took care of that while I was gone."

"How could she do that?" Karen queried, frowning.

"The law makes special considerations for a woman whose husband is convicted and sent to prison. She can divorce him!"

Kyle put steady eyes on her and waited for her reaction to this information. Her eyes studied his face. They searched *his* eyes, traced his strong features, then searched his eyes again.

"I don't believe that, Mr. Rivers," she whispered.

"I don't make a habit of lying," he said.

"No, I didn't mean that. I meant that you're not the kind of man who would do anything dastardly enough to be sent to prison! I don't know you—that's true, but I know dishonesty and cruelty and all the things that children show openly that grownups hide. It shows, things leave their mark, but what I see in you is bitterness and a kind of anger that frightens me. But you're not a criminal!"

"Thank you for that," he said.

"It sounds like you've decided to stay around here since you're going to be watching out for Danny."

"I have to stay another month at least. I got arrested last night, and was sentenced this morning to work for Rolf Schweeney for three weeks."

"What in the world for?"

"In an attempt to silence the wrathful sermon in the street yesterday, I borrowed Tritch's bear hide and spooked Rolf's horses. The results of that led to the demolition of Rolf's wagon. Julian threw me in jail."

"You? You did that?" Suddenly Karen covered her mouth and stifled a giggle. She stood up and came around the desk. "No wonder you like boys. You're a boy yourself," she said, laughing.

He was looking at her. It was the same look that she had seen on his face in the loft. It sobered her smile and drew her to him with an uncanny power. Karen found the strength to look away, but that was the only physical resistance she could muster.

"No, not here," she whispered.

His arms fit perfectly around her and pulled her to him. It was the place she was meant to be, a comforting and peaceful place. If there had been the strength in her to struggle against it, she did not have the will to. Karen bowed her head and laid it against his chest, over his heart. She felt the strength in him and heard the pound of his heart as he lowered his head and then untwined an arm and put his fingers under her chin. He lifted her lips to meet his and kissed her softly.

He released her and gently pushed her to arm's length. She opened her eyes and looked up at him. They became aware at the same moment that they were not alone, and turned their heads to look into the faces of her pupils, who stood inside the doorway staring at them.

Karen took on an intense shade of scarlet and turned toward the blackboard. Kyle set his jaw and shook his head. It took a few moments before Karen could turn and face her students.

"Why?" she asked despairingly. "You've never before come into this room one second before recess was over. Why today?"

"Well," Simeon said, unable to suppress a grin, "we just thought maybe Mr. Rivers would shoot for us. We didn't know you and Mr. Rivers were gonna . . . well, were gonna kiss and all that. We didn't know you was sweethearts, Miss McLaughlin."

"*Were* sweethearts, not *was*, Simeon," she said, then blushed again in a shade darker than before. "We aren't sweethearts!" she said defensively.

"You mean you were kissing him when you don't like him?" Simeon teased.

"Well, no. I do like him . . . I mean I—" She looked helplessly at Kyle and gestured futilely with her hands. "Can't you help me?" she whispered.

"You're doing all right," he said with a grin.

"Mr. Rivers!" she whispered angrily. "This is your fault, so please come up with an explanation!"

"Yes, ma'am," he said. The devil danced in his eyes as he turned to the youngsters. "Miss McLaughlin wouldn't kiss a stranger. She's kissed me before."

Karen's mouth dropped open for a moment, somehow matching up with the astonished look in her eyes. In an instant she recovered, and quickly walked over to the desk and sat down behind it.

"You will all go outside until recess is over. Please leave the room."

The youngsters scrambled outside again, giggling

and blushing, some covering their mouths with a hand. Others, mostly the older boys, winked and grinned as they shot looks back over their shoulders. Inside the schoolroom, the silence became tense for several moments, then Karen addressed Kyle very stiffly:

"Mr. Rivers, my contract states specifically that I cannot have gentlemen callers. I will probably lose my job over this, and you have made it more probable by refusing to clarify things."

"Ma'am, I can't undo this any more than I can unring a bell. Once aboard a bronc, about all a feller can do is ride it out the best he can."

"I shouldn't have let you come in here. I shouldn't have let you do that. Why did I let you do that? I don't want to lose my job!"

"Why would you agree to a contract that required such a thing?"

"Because teaching is my career and I had no intention of ever allowing that. The clause is the usual thing in a teaching contract for women teachers."

"You never intended to allow a man to kiss you?"

"No, definitely not, Mr. Rivers."

"Are you saying you've never been kissed?" Kyle asked skeptically.

"When I was a girl in school, but not since I became a teacher. I am supposed to set an example, and I've adhered strictly to the rules and done my job well. Now, in one big swoop, you've managed to destroy the reputation I have worked so hard to build."

"I'm sorry, Miss McLaughlin," Kyle said.

"You should be sorry, coming in here and—"

"No, ma'am. I'm sorry to hear you haven't allowed yourself to be kissed. Good day, Miss McLaughlin."

Kyle left the school in long strides. He crossed the yard area and motioned to the older boys, who were watching him from under the shade of a large tree. As he untied his mount, the boys gathered around.

"Miss McLaughlin's contract says that if word of this gets around, she'll be required to leave her teaching job here, and I hope you don't want that. I figure it's you older boys' responsibility to keep the little ones quiet about this, you hear?"

Kyle touched his hat as he spun round and cantered away from the school. In one way, the way that might cost Karen her job, he was sorry to have been caught kissing her. In another way, he didn't care if the whole community knew that he'd kissed beautiful Karen McLaughlin.

It was a few hours before sunset when Danny seemed to materialize from out of a dark shadow in the livery barn. Kyle was resetting the shoes on his horse, and at the sudden appearance of the youngster, the black shied and snorted, almost pulling loose from Kyle's grip.

"I reckon a man ought to speak to a horse before he just pops into sight," Kyle drawled, continuing to work at the shoeing as if Danny's presence were expected.

Kyle let down the horse's hoof and went to a can full of nails. He placed a handful of horseshoe nails in the folded cuff of his pants leg and, returning to the black, lifted another hoof between his knees.

"Well, did you think it out?" he asked as he pounded a nail through and bent over the end. He glanced at Danny, then went back to his chore.

"Yes, sir," Danny answered quietly.

"Well?"

"I reckon just having a place to sleep and eat was all right when I lived at Mrs. Brown's, but I'm on my own now. If you'll pay me twenty-five cents a week and my bed and food, I'll take the job."

Kyle hesitated momentarily, and a slight smile crossed his lips. He continued to finish nailing the shoe on the hoof. Then he set down the horse's leg, straightened up, and studied Danny thoughtfully.

"I reckon a man needs some money," Kyle said.

The light in the doorway to the livery flicked briefly as the sheriff strolled inside. Danny backed away a few steps, his attention shifting fearfully between the sheriff and Kyle.

"Afternoon, Sheriff," Kyle said quickly, watching Danny. "Do you know my new hand, Danny Brown?"

Julian was a sharp man, and took the lead handed him. "Yes, I know Danny. You say he's working for you?"

"Yep."

"Well, is he going to school?"

"Yep," Kyle answered.

"He ain't sleeping out in the bushes somewhere, is he?"

"Nope, he'll be staying at the boardinghouse."

"Well, then, Mr. Rivers, I'd say you got yourself a real good hand there."

The sheriff turned and left the livery. Whatever the purpose of his visit, he had put it aside in an effort not to spook Danny.

Kyle finished the shoeing while Danny watched in silence. Kyle started to put away the tools, and then purposely left them on the ground. He led the black to his stall and tied him by the head to the manger.

"Danny, those tools go in a box down by the feed bin. I reckon you can figure out where they go. Supper is at six o'clock over at the boardinghouse. I'll see you then."

In the boardinghouse, he arranged for Danny's meals and secured for him the bunk next to his own. Then he strolled out on the boardwalk and sat down in a chair, waiting for mealtime to roll around.

Danny suddenly appeared from between two buildings. He ambled up with his thumbs stuck in his ragged pants pockets and scrambled onto the chair beside Kyle's. After a few minutes of copying Kyle's observance of the dusty street and the people coming and going, Danny turned to him and said:

"Mr. Rivers, am I a hired hand or a pardner?"

"What would you prefer?" Kyle asked.

"I'd rather be a pardner."

The sun began to dip behind the buildings, causing long shadows in the street. Kyle got to his feet with a moist ache in his eyes but a gentle smile on his lips.

"Let's go eat, pardner," he said. He stepped out in half strides so that Danny's short legs could keep up with him.

Chapter Six

ROLF Schweeney turned out to be a hard man to work for. At first Kyle had thought that three weeks wouldn't be much return to Schweeney for his wagon and team, but after the first twelve-hour day and the kind of labor that brought back memories of the chain gang, Kyle was positive that his taskmaster would get every bit owed to him in those three weeks. What controlled Kyle and made him loyal to the task was his belief in always paying a debt, and in this case he owed Schweeney fair and square.

That first evening on the farm, as Kyle cinched up his saddle to ride to town, young Simeon Schweeney stood nearby watching in silence. Then Rolf came by leading a harnessed mule and scowled at the two of them.

"Simeon, grab that saw and file and sharpen the

teeth while you're resting. Mr. Rivers, I'll see you at sunup.''

Rolf continued leading the mule toward the barn as Simeon picked up the saw and file. The boy grinned at Kyle and shot a look at his father's back as he began filing on the saw teeth.

''My father loves work more than money. He says work keeps a man too busy to find time to get into trouble. I reckon it works for him, but I always seem to be in trouble though I work harder than anybody I know...except him.'' Simeon grinned again and watched his father disappear through the barn door.

''How do you feel about your dad?'' Kyle inquired, mounting his horse.

''He's the finest man I know, Mr. Rivers.''

Kyle nodded approvingly. ''I reckon that's why he's raised a fine son.''

Almost an hour later Kyle rode into Cedar Point and dismounted at the livery. Danny was waiting with a glow to his cheeks and excitement in his eyes.

''I went to school today.''

''Everything go all right?''

''Yes. It was just like it used to be, only I got behind when I was gone. But Miss McLaughlin said she'd help me on Saturday if I wanted. Mr. Rivers...?''

''What?''

''I'm glad you and Miss McLaughlin are sweethearts.''

Kyle clenched his jaw and scowled beyond Danny for a while. ''Did *I* ever tell you that?'' he said finally.

"No, sir."

"Did Miss McLaughlin tell you that?"

"No, sir."

"Then don't repeat it."

Kyle handed Danny the reins and left the boy to his chores. Julian Roman was making his way toward Kyle as Kyle strode down the boardwalk, so he leaned back against a porch post and nodded to the lawman as he came up.

"Evening, Sheriff."

"Got a few minutes, Rivers?"

"I reckon. What's on your mind?"

"Karen McLaughlin seemed to think you were looking for two men. Since it's evident that Jeb Grosse didn't take a shot at you, nor did he accidentally drop a handful of shells or ride your horse in the middle of the night, I assume there's another person and you know who that person might be."

Julian studied him rather intently, and Kyle allowed him his scrutiny, but Kyle kept silent.

"Who else are you looking for, Rivers?"

"I'm doing my time for your court, Sheriff."

"But you're looking too, aren't you?"

"You'll have to guess the answer to that."

The two men exchanged looks for a moment. As Kyle started to walk away, Julian put a restraining hand on his shoulder.

"Talk to me, Rivers!"

Kyle took a deep breath, then looked down at the

hand on his shoulder. "Move your hand, Sheriff," he said softly but forcefully. Julian complied, but didn't back down from Kyle's eyes. The danger in Kyle tamed, and as he spoke, his lips were tight and his words bitter: "There are some things a man can't talk about. I'm asking you to leave it there."

Kyle resumed down the street and turned into Henry Tritch's store. He drank a cup of coffee with the few farmers who were there and then went back to the boardinghouse. Supper was well under way when he seated himself at the table between Danny and Brownlin. His recent words with the sheriff intensified the importance of his mission here in Cedar Point and pulled him back into a shell that kept the world at a distance. It took only a few minutes for the other diners to realize that his mood was anything but friendly, and they avoided him.

Later, after the lamps had been out for a long while in the sleeping room, Kyle lay awake and stared into the darkness. The events of the last three days had kept his thoughts off his reason for being here. What were his plans now? Jeb Grosse's death had numbed him for a while, but, yes, there was another person who was the object of his anger. Where was she?

The sheriff had repeated his own thoughts. The fact that the same frameup had been attempted told Kyle that she was here. He grimaced in the dark, but couldn't temper the bitterness that had leaped into full flame inside him. She had been his wife. When he was framed and sent to prison, he had had no idea that Betsy was in on it until he returned from prison and found that she had left town with Jeb Grosse. And now, the same dastardly deed had almost been repeated, and there was only one person who could be guilty, and she was here in Cedar Point.

"Mr. Rivers?" came a voice from the bed beside him.

Kyle didn't want to be pulled from his thoughts, and he declined an answer, but Danny spoke to him again.

"Mr. Rivers?"

"What?" Kyle growled.

"I won't never repeat what I said."

Kyle recalled what the boy had said down at the livery, but wondered why that would keep a small boy awake at night. A few more minutes passed.

"I swear I won't," Danny whispered.

"So?" Kyle asked, curious about Danny's concern over that small incident.

"Can I still take care of your horse?"

"I didn't know you weren't gonna do it anymore," Kyle answered, totally confused by Danny's words.

"I thought you was mad," Danny said.

Kyle thought this out at length before he answered. Somehow, Danny thought that he was allowed to make only one mistake.

"Did I tell you not to take care of my horse?"

"No, sir."

"Well, I made an agreement with you and I'll stick

to it, the same as I expect *you* to stick to it. You're gonna make mistakes, and I might get mad about it, but you take that in stride. The agreement stays as it is until we both decide that the deal is over. You can depend on that.''

The silence hung for a long while, then Danny ventured again: "How long do you stay mad?"

"I didn't stay mad."

"But you ain't said a word to me since you got mad because I said you and Miss McLaughlin was sweethearts."

The sleeping room fairly exploded. Kyle could hear Brownlin trying to stifle laughter, and the snorting and snickering at Kyle's end of the room resembled the squeals and snorts of a pen of pigs rather than a roomful of men. Suddenly it got unbelievably quiet except for a chuckle in the darkness.

Kyle might as well have been kicked in the chest by an ox. Immediately he seemed to be out of air, and he pulled in a few deep gulps that didn't help in the least. Danny's words left him as short of vocabulary as he was of air. He choked on nothing and the laughter ripped loose again.

"Good grief," he managed to mutter under his breath.

There was nothing to be said. Kyle rolled over to his side and covered his head with the pillow to help shut out the comments that drifted across the room. About the time that silence again dominated the darkness, Danny's small voice pierced his ears:

"Mr. Rivers?"

"Criminy, Danny, shut up!" Kyle bellowed.

"Yes, sir!"

By the time Saturday rolled around, Kyle had begun to change his mind about Rolf Schweeney. Once Kyle got accustomed to the hard work that Rolf seemed to love, it wasn't as bad as it had appeared the first day. Rolf ordered a halt at noon Saturday, and Kyle ate lunch with the family before riding back to town.

It was during this meal that he realized that he actually enjoyed working for Schweeney, not so much that he took to farm work but that it was good not to be driven hour after hour by unrest. The work took his mind totally away from his vengeance, and at the moment he welcomed the interlude of peace.

But that afternoon, instead of heading for town, he turned his horse toward the river to take a look at Widow Brown's cabin. The man who had murdered her must be linked with the woman he sought, because the shells had been planted there.

The door was not locked, so Kyle invited himself in. He spent over an hour in the cabin, searching for he knew not what, but not disturbing anything. In a small room off the pantry, he found a dresser with clothes that would fit Danny. Kyle took these and stuffed them in his saddlebags.

The cabin had turned up no clues. He untied his horse and started to mount, but paused as he looked across the seat of the saddle to a clearing on a hillside. A rider sat there on a sorrel horse, but because of the distance, Kyle could not tell if the rider was watching him or something else.

Without changing his position, he slipped his right hand into the saddlebags and pulled out his spyglass. He focused it on the rider in time to see the horse spun around and spurred to under the cover of the trees. There was something else he noticed. The rider was not a man.

He quickly put back the glass and mounted the black, sent the horse speedily across the meadow into the roaring river, crossed, and then climbed out on the far bank. Less than a half hour later, he held his horse by the reins and knelt down, closely examining the tracks left by the woman's horse. He was an expert tracker, and the signs he read in the dirt might as well have been explanations written on paper.

He had a gut feeling that it was Betsy who had been watching him, but her reasons totally escaped him. If she knew he was in Cedar Point, why hadn't she fled? Why had she gone to the trouble of having his shells planted at the scene of a murder and his horse ridden in the night when her total silence and hiding might have made him move on, still searching for her?

He looked out across the valley and saw the widow's cabin down by the river. There was a connection here or else Betsy wouldn't have been watching him at the cabin. Then again, he was only guessing. Maybe the woman wasn't whom he thought.

Kyle mounted and followed the tracks left by the sorrel. The afternoon dwindled away as he followed the trail, which zigzagged so that it was obvious the rider suspected being tracked and was trying to lose any pursuer. The one thing it did accomplish was to use up daylight before he found where they led to.

He considered camping there and taking up the trail at daybreak, but tomorrow was Sunday and he was sentenced to church. Also, Danny would be waiting at the livery and he didn't want to worry the boy. The tracks would still be there tomorrow afternoon, and he'd resume his search then. He turned his mount toward town.

Sunday morning began normally, but with the arrival of buggies and wagons for church services, Kyle began to feel an uneasiness in his gut, and the closer it got to churchtime, the worse he felt. The truth of the matter was that he had never been inside a church except to be married to Betsy, and that had been one of the most frightening events in his life.

Suddenly he knew he couldn't face it, and he made a beeline for the livery about an hour before the services started. His intention was to saddle up and ride out for the day, but when he arrived at the stall, his horse was not there. He scrutinized the livery, turning slowly in his tracks. There, on the top of two barrels, sat Jory Breene and Brownlin with their arms crossed and smiles on their faces.

"Were you going somewhere, Mr. Rivers?" Jory Breene asked tauntingly.

"Horse stealing is a hanging offense, fellers," Kyle retorted.

"Well, we kinda thought that shirking your sentence rates about the same punishment," Jory answered.

"I'm not going in there," Kyle informed them bluntly.

"Oh, but you are, even if we have to carry you," Jory said. He hopped off the barrel with tight fists, grinning with anticipation.

"You'll regret trying that," Kyle warned.

"Regret? Regret a fight? Double up your dukes, Mr. Fast Gun, because I can black your eyes," Jory goaded.

"Now hold on, Jory," Brownlin said. He walked over to his friend and grasped him by the arm. "We're supposed to escort him, not cripple him. Mr. Rivers, I think you would lose less face by coming along willingly than by showing up in the front pew with your eyes black. Besides, when Miss McLaughlin cooked breakfast yesterday, we relayed your message. You wouldn't want to disappoint her."

Kyle felt the same loss of air as in the sleeping room last night after Danny's oration, and he almost choked again. "What message?" he rasped, not really wanting to hear it.

"That you had promised Danny that she would accompany you both to church this morning. By the way, she arrived at the boardinghouse about a half hour ago, and she's making Danny scrub up and put on his Sunday best. If you get in this here little scuffle with us, you're gonna get real mussed up.''

Kyle seethed. It was a case of pure deviltry from the boardinghouse bunch, and it was going to come to a halt right now. He wasn't against a little horseplay, but neither did he intend to be the brunt of their pranks. And on top of that, the dread of church put him in an ornery mood.

"Then I reckon you two are gonna look as purty as I do.'' Kyle loosened the strap from around his thigh and unbuckled his gun belt. He hung the weapon over a spike in the barn. "If you'll hang on a minute, I'll get Danny in here to whip you, Jory. He's about your size.''

Jory Breene might well have been blown from a cannon. He landed in the middle of Kyle like a rabid badger, but Kyle had closely observed his tactics when he'd fought with Brownlin, and Jory quickly found that Kyle kept him out on the end of his fists. Jory couldn't get in close enough to hurt Kyle, but Kyle was hurting *him*.

"Brownlin!'' Jory yelled. "What in blazes are you doing?''

"I'm watching,'' Brownlin hollered back.

"You're supposed to be helping me! Get in here!''

Kyle continued to keep Jory out of hitting distance, but when he saw Brownlin respond to Jory's cry for help, he knew he'd be hard put to overcome the two of them.

Brownlin had more arm reach than Kyle, but Kyle was ready for him, saving a punch for Brownlin though he pounded Jory with many short jabs to keep him at bay. When Brownlin swung, Kyle threw up a guard arm, but Brownlin followed with a left that Kyle had never seen him use on Jory. It caught Kyle off guard and put him down on the floor of the livery. Jory was on him like a dog on a cat.

Kyle tried to regain his footing, but never managed to accomplish it. Brownlin outweighed Kyle and when he joined Jory in the pileup, Kyle was overpowered and took a sound pounding although his attackers didn't go unscathed.

"That's it! Brownlin, off of him!" ordered Julian Roman. He planted a boot into Jory's backside and at the same time tugged on Brownlin's arm. "Doggone it, Brownlin, you hit him again and I'm gonna arrest you! Get up!"

A quiet seeped through the livery as the dust shifted and settled in the few beams of light that filtered down through the barn. At first Kyle seemed to be unconscious, but then they saw he was only trying to get his bearings before he staggered to his feet. He grasped a timber to help pull himself up.

"Weren't going to church, huh, Rivers?" Julian snapped.

"Still ain't," Kyle grunted.

"Well, Rivers, I hate to have to do this." Julian hollered over his shoulders, "Come on in!"

Schweeney, Tritch, and two huge cowboys entered the livery. Kyle heaved a deep breath and glared at Julian.

"I know when I'm licked," he muttered.

"Figured that you had a little more sense in that head of yours. Jory and Brownlin—you two get cleaned up and meet us at the boardinghouse. You're gonna escort him."

"Well, we ain't going inside," Jory informed Julian, wiping his arm across a gash in his cheek.

"After watching you two the last couple of years, I think you'd both benefit from a sermon. And as deputies you're under orders, and I hereby order you to escort him to a pew!"

At ten minutes before the ten-o'clock service, Kyle Rivers stepped out of the boardinghouse escorted by Jory and Brownlin. All wore clean shirts and they'd been washed and polished, but all three sported at least one black-and-purple eye and multiple swollen bruises on their faces. Karen McLaughlin sat on a chair near the sheriff's office with Danny, waiting for Kyle to show up. She stood up slowly, gripping Danny by the hand, and gaping as the colorful trio came up to her.

"Mr. Rivers! Do you really expect me to accompany you after you've been brawling?" she inquired.

"No, ma'am," he said, and tried to step around her.

"Oh, no! You're going to explain to me right now why you made such a public thing out of my accompanying you this morning and then have the gall to show up like this!"

"Miss McLaughlin, I had nothing to do with that. As I said, we cannot unring a bell, and you fell for a prank. Do as you please, ma'am."

Kyle continued down the street with the other two men. Suddenly Karen caught up with them and slid in beside him, still holding Danny's hand. Kyle stopped and looked down at her.

"I am pleased to accompany you, Mr. Rivers," she said. As he started to protest, she shook her head and smiled lightly. "Please, don't say no."

A grin appeared briefly on his lips, and then he took her by the arm. As they walked to the church, Danny stumbled often at Karen's side, because he was staring intently from Kyle to Karen.

It was the reverend's custom to greet the congregants at the doorway as they came in. He tensed as the five of them approached. Kyle and Karen stopped in front of him and merely looked at him, neither having anything to say. The preacher, on the other hand, wasn't sure how to greet this group, and he chewed his lip as he studied Kyle's face and then Jory's and Brownlin's. He finally cleared his throat and looked down at Danny.

"And whom have you brought to church today, Danny?"

"You know Miss McLaughlin, my teacher," Danny said. "And this is Mr. Rivers, my pardner." He seemed struck with indecision suddenly. A worried look settled into his eyes as he chanced a look at Kyle and then one at Karen. "But they don't like each other," he added.

Kyle immediately managed a cough, and he firmly guided Karen around the preacher and into the church. He heard Brownlin chuckle, but he silenced that with a swift look over his shoulder. The four grown-ups ignored the stares as they made their way to the front and sat down in an empty pew. It was hard to get there, but the front pew had its advantages. Kyle didn't have to look anybody in the eye and all they could see was his back, which suited him just fine.

The afternoon sun warmed his back as Kyle leaned out from his saddle and studied the tracks. An eagle screeched and he looked up into the blue overhead. Then the morning's services came to mind and he shuddered, still feeling a little weak from the strain of it all. He put his attention back on the tracks and nudged his horse forward.

The tracks neared the river again, but this time, instead of crossing directly as they had done several times before, they cut a diagonal path toward the water and entered the river in a manner that made it look as if the horse would continue upstream. Kyle saw rugged rapids not far up the waterway. The trail was laid to throw him off, but it was evident that the animal had to go downstream.

Nearly a half mile farther down the river, the tracks came out, as Kyle suspected they would. The tracking was easy now, because the rider rode confidently in a straight line, and, coming to a trail, followed it. Kyle rode up to a gate with a sign that warned it was Bolden property and to keep out. The woman on the horse was apparently not Betsy but Queenie Bolden herself.

Kyle turned back and headed toward town. In a way, he was relieved. The fire of revenge was hot enough in him to scorch out lives, but there was also the memory of a woman he had loved. What would he actually do when he caught up with her? He had intended to kill Jeb Grosse to satisfy his revenge, but what of Betsy? The bitter thing in him was fed constantly by the memory that his woman had discarded him for another man, and he believed that when they met again, his rage would be beyond control.

The sun disappeared behind the horizon and the light waned as Kyle rode into Cedar Point. The town seemed overly quiet, but then it was Sunday evening. He dismounted and looked around for Danny, but didn't find him, so he unsaddled and rubbed down the black himself. He threw a few forkfuls of hay into the manger and dumped a can of oats in the box. Then he strolled out into the street.

Something was wrong. Not a soul walked the boardwalks, and the few lights that glowed were only in the saloon and Tritch's store. The tie racks were full with saddled horses both at the saloon and at the store. Kyle walked cautiously toward Tritch's place.

"Mr. Rivers!" Danny called out from between two buildings. "Get off the street!"

Kyle sensed the urgency in his voice and quickly melted in between the buildings and hurried to where he'd heard Danny's voice.

"What's up, Danny?"

"Sheriff Roman got shot!"

"How bad? Who shot him?"

"Simeon Schweeney!"

"Where's the sheriff now?"

"In the saloon. The cowboys have got him, and they already got the doctor in there."

"Stay hid," Kyle ordered.

He crossed the street and worked his way toward the saloon. Through the windows of Tritch's store, Kyle could see a large gathering of men with rifles. He slipped around to the back of the saloon and went in through the rear entrance, inspecting the interior from behind a door before he stepped into view.

"Look out! There's their hired gun!"

"Hold your fire!" Kyle bellowed.

"Hold your fire!" somebody repeated.

"I just rode into town and I'd sure like to know what's going on," Kyle said.

"Somebody shot Rolf Schweeney, and the farmers figure we did. Rivers, there ain't a man here that knows a thing about it and we'll all swear to that, but they're about to get more lead back than they're sending!"

"Where's the sheriff?"

"Right over here."

Several men moved aside, and Kyle saw Julian on

a table with the doctor bending over him. Kyle went over and asked about his condition.

"He's gonna make it," the doctor said.

Kyle studied Julian's unconscious face, and then he looked around and announced to all the cowboys in the room, "I told you before, and this is the last time I'm telling you. I'm no hired gunfighter. I don't work for the farmers."

"What are you doing here, then?" a man asked.

"What are *you* doing here?" he questioned back.

"Well, seems I'm living here for a while."

"Same here." Kyle looked the cowboys over again. "Where's Mr. Bolden?"

"I heard the queen has got ornery as a she-bear and most of his men have quit him," the man said. "I figure he's got so much work that he can't leave."

"Who shot the sheriff?"

"That kid of Schweeney's. The boy's out of his head over his dad. We don't know what happened out there, and for sure *we* didn't have anything to do with it. The sheriff was in here when that kid rode into town throwing lead at the saloon. Then he ran into the store and we could hear him yelling that we shot his father. Well, the kid started shooting toward the saloon here again until he ran out of ammunition. Julian went out to get ahold of him, but the kid yanked out another gun. We managed to help Julian back in here, and the farmers came out and wrestled the kid back into the store."

"I was coming on the run to find out if Schweeney was dead or needed medical attention," the doctor said, pausing in his treatment of Julian. "But the kid shot Julian before I could find out how bad his dad was. Think you can get over there and find out?"

Kyle let his eyes settle over the group of cowboys again. Every one of them was armed, and Kyle knew that when they decided to return the farmers' fire, there would be dead men on both sides.

"Has anybody tried to make peace?" he asked.

"Of course not," answered the man who'd spoken earlier. "Every time we poke our noses near the door, they plant some lead over here. So we're gonna send a little back!"

Kyle walked over to the swinging door and pushed it with his hand. As the door flapped, a slug buried itself against the outside of the building.

"Hold your fire!" he hollered.

"You ain't getting no peace now, you cow chaser!" Jory Breene yelled as another slug buried itself nearby.

"Breene, cool down!" Kyle hollered.

Breene was silent for a moment. "Is that you, Rivers?"

"Yes, and hold your fire. I'm coming over."

It was quiet again. "Only you, Rivers. Nobody else."

Kyle looked back at the cowboys in the saloon before he stepped out onto the boardwalk. "You say you don't want a war. I reckon you could avoid one and pull a fast one at the same time by just kinda melting out that back door. The fellers across the street would feel mighty sheepish hiding from an empty saloon. Just a suggestion. Otherwise, do as you please. I'm not on any side.'' Kyle stepped through the swinging doors.

Chapter Seven

KYLE sweated a little as he made a target of himself in front of the saloon. Then he stepped down into the street and crossed. As he entered the store, several rifles were rammed against him.

"I'm gonna find a box to fit your carcass yet," Rube hissed, poking his gun barrel against Kyle's neck. "What were you doing in there with the cowboys?"

"Trying to find out what's going on."

"Have you been working for them all this time and spying on us?" Jory demanded.

"They were just accusing me of doing about the same for you folks. I sure wish somebody'd make up my mind." Kyle allowed his words to sink in before he went on. "The doc sent me on an errand," he finished quietly.

Slowly the rifles lowered and a low discussion began

around the room. Looking for Simeon, Kyle saw him slumped in a chair and holding his head in his hands.

"Excuse me," he said, attempting to make his way toward Simeon, but a man pressed a rifle hard against his chest. Kyle stared the man down, pushed the rifle aside, and walked over to Simeon. The boy knew he was there, but turned his gaze around the room in an effort to avoid his penetrating but patient scrutiny. Suddenly Simeon slapped his hands down on his knees, groaned in frustration, and sprang to his feet.

"I didn't mean to shoot the sheriff! I don't know what happened! It just happened!"

"Tell me about your dad," Kyle said softly.

"The cowboys shot him! I saw him fall out of the wagon and lie on the ground with his head bleeding." Simeon slammed his fists together. "I saw the cowboy hat on the man that shot. It wasn't no farmer. It was a cowboy that killed him!" Simeon shut his eyes and heaved several deep breaths. "I shot the sheriff, but I swear I didn't mean to. Did you see him, Mr. Rivers? Please don't say he's dead!"

"He's not dead," Kyle answered.

The boy sighed with relief. He slumped down in a chair and put his head in his hands.

"I want you to take the doc and me out to your dad, Simeon."

"Hold on a minute, Rivers!" Tritch roared. "There's an army of cowboys out there just waiting for one of us to stick his head out of here. You're not taking that boy into any more danger."

"Speaking of holding on a minute, Tritch," Kyle said coolly, "why don't the bunch of you take a few and calm down? I don't believe the cowboys are to blame in this. None of the cowboys in that saloon know any more than you do. Come on, Simeon."

No one stopped them as Kyle led Simeon out onto the boardwalk. He gazed across the street, and from what he could see, the saloon looked empty, which he considered a blessing. Then they quickly crossed the street, and Kyle stepped inside and motioned to the doctor. Moments later they led Simeon's horse down to the livery, where Kyle and the doctor saddled. Then the three of them rode out into the night.

As the trio approached the farmhouse, a warning shot rang out. They pulled up their horses in the darkness.

"Who's there?" a woman's voice hollered.

"It's me, Mother—Simeon!"

The door swung open and the lamplight flooded the path as Mrs. Schweeney hurried out from the house. Simeon dismounted and put an arm around her.

"Your father's in the house, Simeon. Go talk to him. He's so worried you ran off and got in trouble. Go on. He needs to see you."

"He's alive!" Simeon exclaimed.

"Yes. He was hit in the head. But about all it did was knock him out and make an ugly cut. He'll be fine, son. Go see him."

Kyle breathed a sigh of relief and watched Simeon

make a dash for the door. Then he leaned over from his saddle and started to speak to Mrs. Schweeney as the doctor dismounted and tied his horse.

"I want to examine him," the doctor said.

"Thank you. I'd feel better if you would." She put her attention back on Kyle. "You were about to say something."

"The boy did get himself in trouble, ma'am, but I reckon that's between you folks and the sheriff. Did you see who fired the shot?"

"It was a cowboy, Mr. Rivers. That's all I saw. It was a cowboy. Last week there was a note wedged in the door that warned Rolf to run you off or pay the consequences. He ignored the threat. When it's daylight, I can show you where the man shot from, if that will help any."

"Yes, ma'am, that will probably help."

"Why didn't the sheriff come out here, Mr. Rivers? He should've come."

"You'll have to ask Simeon about that, ma'am."

Kyle headed back toward town. The war had barely been avoided tonight. He wondered how long it would be before it broke out in full scale. Then he forced the problem from his mind. It was Julian's affair, not his. Except, perhaps, for the note on the door.

The next morning Kyle showed up at the Schweeneys' at daybreak. Instead of working the fields, he followed Simeon to the spot where the rider had been. After sending the boy back to the farm, he crouched and studied the hoofprints. Then he shoved back his hat and let out a long whistle. The tracks were the same ones he had followed yesterday. It appeared that Queenie was wading right into a range war. Evidently she was assuming that his presence at Rolf's farm meant that the farmers had hired his gun. He mounted and followed the tracks. Then again, there was the possibility that someone else could have been riding the same horse that Queenie rode yesterday.

The hoofprints repeated the zigzag style that yesterday's had displayed, a fact that told Kyle it was the same rider on the horse. Suddenly the prints struck out in a straight line and went onto the main road from Cedar Point, quickly becoming obscure among the many other tracks. He returned to Rolf's farm and finished out the day in the fields.

That evening, after he'd eaten at the boardinghouse, Kyle visited Julian's bedside and told him what had happened since he was shot. Julian seemed in good spirits as he listened, but he winced occasionally.

"You're hurting," Kyle commented.

"Yeah," Julian grumbled. "And I can't afford to be. I've got a war brewing!"

"I'd like to say that your deputies, Jory and Brownlin, could handle things, but they're both on the same side and Jory sure isn't a man of peace."

"That's a bit of gospel, Rivers. What I need is a man that can handle hot lead, hotheads, and fistfights, and also be fair and above it all.'' Suddenly Julian's eyes took on a shrewd glow that wasn't wasted on Kyle. ''You once said, 'If you ever need a gun.' Well, Rivers, I need a gun!''

''No! Absolutely not!''

''You mean that was offered only for when *you* want to, not when *I* might need you.''

''No. I meant when you yourself need help, not when your job needs help. I won't represent the law!''

''Doggone it, Rivers, you would represent *me!* It wouldn't hurt you for just a couple of days, and I really need you!''

They eyed each other sharply. Julian wavered first and let out a sigh. ''I can't even stare you down. I'm in just miserable shape. Dang it, Rivers! There ain't anybody else in this town that can handle the job if there's real trouble—not even for an hour!''

Kyle took a deep breath and let it out in a soft hiss. He grinned as he shook his head. ''Julian, I'm gonna regret this, but all right. But there's one thing I won't budge on. I won't sport a star on my chest, and that's final!''

Julian grinned back. ''It won't hurt you, but if you don't want anybody to see it, stick it on your undershirt. That way, if you get backed in a corner you can prove you've got the authority.''

''I don't wear an undershirt,'' Kyle grumbled.

''Well, maybe you better start wearing one, because you have to have that badge on your person, and that's about the best I can suggest since you're ashamed to wear it on the outside!''

Kyle rode to Schweeney's and worked out a temporary release from his work sentence. Rolf was agreeable, but upset about what was going to happen to Simeon. He tried to get an answer from Kyle about it, but Kyle told him it was up to Julian. It was near noon when he returned to Cedar Point.

As he entered the town, he saw several horses tied in front of the saloon, one of which was the sorrel horse he'd been tracking. He left his black in the livery, then made his way down the boardwalk and stepped down into the street beside the sorrel. He lifted its left foreleg and studied the shoe, noting the two nails on one side and three on the other.

Suddenly he tensed and slowly let down the horse's hoof, barely breathing at the feel of an iron barrel rammed against his side. He straightened and looked into Bolden's eyes, glaring into his, only inches away.

''You're trespassing,'' Bolden hissed, putting more weight against the revolver that jabbed Kyle's waist.

''I didn't know this was your horse,'' Kyle answered carefully.

''Now you do, Rivers, and if you breathe wrong, you'll give me reason to shoot. What do you think you're doing?''

''I've been tracking a horse, and I thought this was the one.''

"Well, it ain't, because he ain't been out of the corral in a week and I'm the only one that rides him."

Kyle knew better, but kept the fact to himself. "Then excuse me, Bolden. My mistake."

"Your mistake was taking on the job with the farmers. I know how to take care of your kind, and mister, it's about to be your last mistake!"

Bolden backed a couple feet away, but he held the gun on Kyle. The rancher's expression showed not anger or hate but the promise to back up his words.

For Kyle to attempt an explanation would be words wasted on the cattleman. He held his silence and waited for Bolden to make the next move, constantly watching the man's eyes, and aware that Bolden wanted him to make a move that would give him a reason to pull the trigger.

"Turn your back to me and cross the street, Rivers," the cattleman ordered.

The minute Kyle turned his back on Bolden, he felt his .45 lifted from the holster.

"Walk, gunfighter," Bolden snarled.

Kyle walked casually, hoping not to catch the eye of the townspeople, but they were aware of the confrontation between him and Bolden. He stepped up on the boardwalk across the street and turned around, watching the gray-haired rancher.

"Rivers," Bolden hollered, "I'll leave your peashooter in the saloon."

Kyle burned within. Bolden was a man who knew

how to profit from public opinion, and at the moment he was flaunting the fact that he'd gotten the drop on Kyle. There wasn't a lot to do about the situation at the moment, so Kyle settled down into a chair and watched to see how far Bolden would push his small victory, but the man took it no further and went into the saloon.

At that moment, the weekly stage rumbled and jingled as the teams pulled the swaying coach down the street and halted at the door of the boardinghouse, which served as a station for the stage line. Two men got off. One hurried into the boardinghouse, but the other leaned back against the outer wall and surveyed the town.

Only twice in his travels had Kyle run into a man like the one watching the town. The fellow was starkly out of place, emitting an air of coldness that made Kyle tense. He wore a long coat, but the bulge just below his waistline told Kyle what he already knew—the man was a professional gun. When he saw Bolden make his way down the walk and shake hands with the man, Kyle knew that Bolden's words were about to be backed up.

The two men talked for a moment, then looked across the street at Kyle. Bolden nodded at something the man said, then the two of them crossed and stood on the walk, blatantly watching him. Almost catlike, the stranger stalked up to within a few steps of Kyle.

''Next time I see you, Rivers, you'd better be wearing a gun,'' the man taunted softly.

"If I am, you'd better not be wearing yours," Kyle taunted back, totally unintimidated.

"You frighten me," the man mocked.

"Then maybe you've got a little sense and you're not all for show," Kyle replied.

The man's lips pulled into tight lines and his eyes narrowed. His nostrils flared slightly, and a slight tremor of controlled disposition almost got out of control. Then he glanced up and down the street and said, "It's a good thing you have a lawman in town to protect your sassy mouth or you'd learn right now I ain't show. Where's your guardian angel at the moment?"

"He's looking right at you," Kyle whispered, and he opened his shirt just far enough to show the badge beneath.

The man's eyes opened a little wider, revealing that Kyle had landed something unexpected on him. The man studied him somberly for a while, and then nodded vaguely. "Like I said. Next time you better be wearing a gun."

The stranger turned back toward Bolden, but Kyle saw Bolden become uneasy as the man approached him. Kyle heard the beginning of the stranger's protest to Bolden:

"You didn't tell me he was your local lawman."

Bolden's features showed confusion. He looked around the stranger to Kyle. Kyle pulled his shirt aside again, but just enough for Bolden's eyes and not the town's. He wasn't boasting the badge; he was merely delighting himself with the shocking effect it had on Bolden and his new gunhand. The cattleman's mouth opened slightly, but nothing came out of it. Abruptly it snapped shut and Bolden nodded toward the horses tied in front of the saloon. A minute later the two men rode out of town.

Kyle stretched and sauntered over to the saloon. He stepped through the swinging doors to be greeted by many jesting faces, and he immediately wondered how far the orneriness would go before he recovered his weapon.

Kyle addressed the bartender: "Say, my gun musta got thirsty, 'cause it sneaked off without me. Any chance it came in here?"

The bartender tried to keep a sober face, but a hearty grin overcame him. He glanced around the room. "What do you say?" he asked the group.

"Aw, give him his gun," somebody said. "I reckon he's lost enough face as it is."

The bartender reached under the counter for the .45 and shoved it toward Kyle.

"It's a good thing you didn't come stomping in here hot and huffy, or you might not have had it back before sundown!"

"That's kinda the way I figured it," Kyle answered, slipping the weapon back into the holster. He allowed a smile to cross his lips as he walked toward the doors. "Thanks, boys," he said, and stepped out onto the walk.

*   *   *

The week passed without more violence. Kyle had never guessed that a lawman did more than walk the streets agitating people, but he soon found that every minute brought another demand on his attention. Four boys put a bag of skunks in the laundryman's basket, and when he opened it up, thinking it was clothes, well . . . And more than a dozen times, skirmishes got out of hand in the saloon. At midnight on Thursday, several cowhands managed to drag a couple of outhouses onto the main street and leave them there. Tritch threw a man who wanted more credit out of his store. Tritch told him to pay up with whatever he had before he came to charge anything more. The man came back and dumped a wheelbarrow full of chicken droppings in the middle of the store, saying it was all he had to pay with. Naturally, a brawl ensued.

By Friday Kyle was about to take the reverend's sermon to heart and pray—pray for Julian's quick recovery. As far as Bolden and his gunhand were concerned, there hadn't been any action from that direction.

Four or five times during the week he saw Karen, but their conversation was always brief. Kyle wasn't pursuing the friendship and neither was she. However, he always watched her and often he caught *her* watching *him*.

Saturday morning came, and Kyle made it a special point to ignore Karen as much as possible at breakfast in the boardinghouse. He was hoping to end the talk about them that Danny had begun. He would be moving on when his business was finished here, and he didn't want to cause her any more trouble with her teaching job than he already had. He wondered how many of the children had told their parents of the incident in the schoolhouse.

As the Saturday sun climbed slowly into the sky, Kyle made several rounds of the town. Just before lunch, he moseyed into the shadowed livery and heard voices from a stall near a window. Edging up on the sounds, he saw Karen and Danny sitting on a pile of clean straw, studying a schoolbook in the beam of sunlight that pierced the darkness of the livery.

"Those are vowels, Danny. They are special because you cannot make a word without at least one of them. Danny? What in heaven's name is on your mind?"

"Oh, I was just thinking about Mrs. Brown," the boy said quietly.

"Try not to think about her, Danny."

"Why not? She taught me lots of things. Why shouldn't I think about her?"

"Oh, I didn't mean that. I thought you were thinking about just the bad day. But if you're thinking about the good times, then, yes, remember them all."

"When you're teaching me like this, I think about her, Miss McLaughlin." Danny was quiet for a while. Then he reached up and brushed at his eyes. "Mrs.

Brown said that God had something better planned for me. I wish she'd have told me before she. . . . Miss McLaughlin, was Mrs. Brown an angel? How'd she know what God plans for me?''

Kyle saw Karen struggle for an answer. She pressed her lips together and swallowed several times, emotion bottling up inside her. Suddenly she reached out and pulled the boy onto her lap and hugged him with her cheek buried in his tousled hair.

"Young man, I don't have those answers for you," she said.

Danny wrapped his arms as far around her as they would wrap, and Kyle saw them tighten and hold.

"I wish you were my mother, Miss McLaughlin," he said.

"I would like that too," she said. Several minutes passed, and then Karen put Danny back where he'd been. He looked up at her.

"How come you can't be my mother?"

"Because I'm alone, Danny. Married people can adopt orphans, but not single women. It's the law, Danny, and it's a good law, because what you need is a family. Let's get back to the lessons." Karen looked at the book, but Kyle saw that she wasn't interested in it. "Danny, you must remember that I am your teacher. We all wish for many things, but they can't all be. I cannot be your mother and you must understand that. Do you?''

"Yes ma'am," he mumbled.

The lesson then continued, and Kyle slowly retreated from hearing distance. Life was tough, but it seemed that some received more than their fair share of toughness. As he went by the sheriff's office, he opened the door and stepped in to chat with Julian, hoping to get Karen and Danny's conversation off his mind. Julian was sitting at the desk, and his movements were very careful.

"You've sure been keeping yourself scarce," Julian muttered, looking at Kyle as he pulled up a chair.

"Jailhouses give me the creeps," Kyle replied, easing against the back of hand-carved oak.

"You'll get over that."

Kyle perked up. "Meaning what?"

"Oh, after a while it won't bring back any memories. In fact, you'll look at it as a refuge from the hysteria out there on the street. I've been known to go in the cell room and sleep there, hoping that somebody would lock the door and throw away the keys so I wouldn't have to deal with everybody's problems anymore."

"Sheriff, my job for you is about through, and I'm looking forward to finishing my sentences in this town. I'm not about to get used to this job!"

"It's steady," Julian murmured, suddenly getting busy with some papers on the desk.

"I'm not looking for a job, steady or otherwise!"

"What *are* you looking for, Kyle?" Julian asked quietly. He peered intently at him.

Kyle pulled his attention from Julian and let his gaze

travel around the room. The fatigue he had felt at finding Jeb Grosse's grave overcame him again.

"Something I lost, Julian," he said with a sigh.

"What if you find it? What are you going to do after that?"

"I guess I'll ride on down the trail until I find out why I'm alive." Kyle got to his feet. "How much longer do you think it'll be before the doc says you're okay?"

"Oh, a couple of—" Suddenly Julian's eyes took on that glow again, the glow that bothered Kyle and made him look sideways at the sheriff. "He hasn't exactly said yet."

"Don't try anything, lawman. I'm on to what you're about to pull here, and it ain't gonna work. If I did take a steady job, it sure in tarnation wouldn't be this one!"

"Once a man lives by the gun, he's married to it," Julian said. "About the only thing you'll do is drift from town to town with that iron on your hip, and one day you'll find a faster gun, and that's the end of that story. You'll never take the iron off, not for love and not for wealth, but you can channel it into something you can live with instead of letting it kill you. There's a job here. Think about it. By the way, why were you looking at Bolden's horse's shoes?"

"That horse was ridden two days in a row by someone. I'm assuming it was Queenie Bolden, and one of those days, the rider on that horse took a shot at Rolf Schweeney."

Julian rubbed his jaw and submerged into deep thought. He lit his pipe, leaned back in his chair, and watched the smoke rings.

"You know, Rivers, something's beginning to come to mind here. If Jeb Grosse planted shells on you, then he must have told that to somebody in order for that trick to be pulled again, along with the other stunts. Now here's my thoughts. Bolden has always been mad at you. Suppose that Jeb told him about you before he died, and Bolden's the one who tried to make it work again to get rid of you. Of course, Bolden surely didn't murder Mrs. Brown—on that I'd bet my job. Bolden isn't made of that kind of stuff, although, on the other hand, he has just hired a professional gun. I don't understand that, but we've got a connection here somewhere and Bolden's sure looking suspicious at the moment."

"Why would Jeb Grosse tell Bolden about the rotten stunt he pulled on me?" Kyle said.

But Julian never got the chance to answer. The door burst open and several farmers plunged into the room.

"Sheriff! Jory Breene's house and barn got burned to the ground by them cowboys, and they dragged timber through his spud patch and killed all his taters! But we got them holed up in a draw, and we already got one of them for you!"

"You *what!*" Julian thundered.

The lawman lurched to his feet, then froze in place with a pained look on his face. He sank back into his chair, his breathing labored. His skin took on a grayish tone, and he struggled inwardly with something, and then finished with a groan. He clenched his jaw and studied the men in helpless anger.

"Where?" he whispered.

"About a mile west of Bolden's spread. You know, where the river splits and goes down the gorge. But you'd better hurry before Jory goes up there alone and gets himself killed!"

Julian exploded in spite of his pain: "Jory Breene ain't one bit more important to me than a cowboy! I don't want a single man killed! I haven't got a side. I've got friends on both sides and enemies on both sides!"

He struggled to his feet and leaned on the desk, supporting himself with one arm as he lifted the other and shook his finger at the farmers.

"And I'll hang Jory for killing a cowboy just as fast as I'd hang a cowboy for shooting him! Now get out of here and go home. If I see your faces when I get up there in that draw, I'll arrest the lot of you. Go home! Now! Git!"

Without any protest, the men left the office. Kyle watched the wounded sheriff painfully lower himself back into the chair. Julian Roman wasn't riding a horse anywhere in his condition, and he rested his eyes on Kyle.

"I need you," he said, his voice barely audible.

"One man can't stop a range war, and I didn't come

here to play sheriff!'' Kyle turned and started toward the door, but Julian's words halted him:

"*I'd* be only one man, and *I'd* go if I could.''

Kyle studied the grain of the wood on the door in front of him. He didn't turn around as Julian's words cut at his pride.

"I need you, Kyle,'' Julian repeated quietly.

Chapter Eight

THE afternoon sun blinked sporadically upon the rugged terrain as a storm pushed clouds over its face. A deep black above the skyline, beneath the purple clouds, foretold a deluge only hours away. Already in turmoil, the wind lashed Kyle's face.

The black horse quickly covered the miles, but time dragged as Kyle urged the beast toward the draw where the river forked. He didn't know what awaited him, but Bolden's gun hand would play a part if his cowboys were holed up. And trying to stop Jory Breene from fighting was as dangerous as kissing a poisonous snake.

"Backed in a corner." Julian's words lurked warningly in Kyle's mind as he sent the black across a meadow. In recent years he had always defied the law, but today he was representing the law. No. Actually, he was only a friend of Julian Roman's. For the law, he wouldn't have lent a hand in this war between cowboy and farmer. But for the man, he would do his best.

Guiding the horse with one hand, he urged the animal up a rugged incline, and with his other hand, he reached inside his shirt and pulled the badge free from its hidden place. He held it in his palm, studying it, and then shook his head. There was a point where a man's stubbornness about his beliefs turned into stupidity, and Kyle was wise enough to know when he had reached that point. He fairly winced as he grimly pinned the star over his heart. Then he riveted his eyes on the trail ahead. He was only one man about to pit himself against many, and the only thing on his side was the authority of the badge.

Kyle slowed his horse when he came upon the dangerous piles of rock beneath a cliff. It was the beginning of the gorge where one fork of the river plunged down toward the lower country. Roaring waterfalls escorted the current as it plunged and fell, spraying into mist and then gathering in swirling pools.

Kyle splashed his horse across the river and came up on the far side. He nudged the black with a spur, and the horse moved out in an easy lope. He was less than a half mile from the draw where the cowboys were pinned down when gunfire cracked from directly ahead and the echoes reverberated in the deep gorge behind him. After taking to some light brush, he came out unnoticed about a half dozen yards from a group of farmers crouched down behind rocks.

Kyle whistled softly, and the men turned their heads as he dismounted and tied his horse near several other mounts. He kept low and moved in beside Henry Tritch. Tritch studied the badge a moment, then scowled and asked, "Is that legal and legitimate?"

"Yep," Kyle answered, scrutinizing the draw ahead. "Where are the cowboys holed up?"

"See that bunch of dead timber by the ledge of rock sticking out over there? Well, there's a cut back in behind, and that's where they've got their horses. The cowboys are nested in the downed timber."

Kyle turned his eyes on Tritch, and the storekeeper slowly stiffened and backed away. Kyle said to him, "I was just wondering if you saw the man that burned down Jory's place and tore out his tater patch?"

"See him?" Tritch exclaimed. "Why, there had to be twenty of them from the damage Jory described."

"Did *you* see him or them?" Kyle demanded.

"Why, no. He told me about it."

"Go home, Tritch."

Kyle crouched over to where the next man hovered protectively behind a boulder. He asked the same question, got the same answer, and ordered the man home. When he got to the last man, he inquired first of the next firing line of farmers, then ordered that man home. Kyle started to move on, but glanced around and observed that not a one of them had made a move to obey him.

Ignoring the men, he passed back through them,

went to his horse, and pulled several pairs of handcuffs from the saddlebags. He then walked over to Tritch and gave him a punch that knocked him down in the weeds beside the rock. Then Kyle quickly wrestled him into submission and cuffed his hands behind him.

"You're under arrest for being a part of a vigilante attempt, Tritch. Of course, you're luckier than some of them are gonna be, because when I run out of handcuffs, I'm gonna start shooting." Kyle registered a threatening look on the group as he spoke, then addressed the nearest man, who happened to be Reuben Sparks, the undertaker. "Do you want cuffs or would you prefer one of them boxes you're always talking about tailoring for me?"

"Neither one, Rivers. I'll get on back to town."

The rest of the men followed Rube's example, and within a few moments they were mounted and riding toward the river. Kyle hauled Tritch to his feet and then cuffed him to a stout bush.

"Aw, come on, Rivers," Tritch said. "I was just seeing if you meant it. Come on, let me go."

"You had your chance to do it right."

Starting up the draw, Kyle quickly found himself the target of gunfire from the cowboys hidden in the fallen timber. He dived in behind a boulder and waited for the barrage to die off before warily peeking around to locate the other farmers. It took a while to work his way over to them.

He quickly located the massive form of Rolf Schweeney. Jory Breene could start a riot, but Rolf was a man who could stop one, not only because of his great size but because he had the respect of his neighbors. As Kyle slid down beside him, Rolf started in surprise, but then he smiled and indicated the piles of timber.

"I haven't seen Bolden and Queenie, but they're up there somewhere. So's that gunman."

"I thought you didn't believe in fighting, Rolf," Kyle said.

"Not if I can avoid it, but both sides must work at peace to have it. Bolden demanded this battle, and now he has it. I figure fighting should be the very last resort, but, as you once said, a man with a family has more reason to fight, and therefore I fight."

"How do you know Bolden is the guilty one?" Kyle asked, starting his strategy on Rolf.

"I saw him and his cowboys."

"You saw Bolden torch Jory's house?"

"No, I saw Queenie torch Jory's house. Bolden and his men were down in the potato patch, dragging logs around and tearing out his fences. I took out for town to find Jory, but met him coming home. By the time we got back to his place, there was nothing left to save." Rolf studied the star on Kyle's shirt for a moment. "I'm sorry that Julian is hurt so bad. He wouldn't have sent you if he could've come himself. I'm sorry my son is the cause of that."

"Then make this whole thing easier on Julian, Rolf. Go home, but first help me get the rest of these farmers out of here. If you're a witness to what happened at Jory's place, then Julian can get Bolden legally, through the law. The result of this fight today will be a lot of dead men, and that would make things as hard on Julian as things could get. Go home!''

Rolf looked down at his weapon, and then peered through the rocks. He settled his gaze back on Kyle.

''Jory will not leave. Not at your threats, not at your orders, not at your pleading. I'm gonna stay because Jory Breene is my neighbor and he's a good friend. Tell me, Mr. Rivers, did you intend to take on Bolden, his cowboys, and his gun hand by yourself after you run all of us off?''

''I reckon I'll take it as it comes, Rolf, but I want you to leave.''

''No. You can't stop Jory without hurting him or maybe killing him. I'm staying, Rivers.''

Kyle reached out and grabbed Rolf's wrist with the intention of cuffing him, but that act relayed a frightful message to Kyle. Grabbing Rolf was like grabbing muscle on a bull. As Kyle released his grip, Rolf flashed a gentle grin and nodded.

''I'm staying. I have an interest in you, Rivers. You still haven't paid for my wagon.'' Rolf's eyes twinkled for a moment. Then they sobered and he peered over the boulder toward the draw. ''Jory has managed to get dangerously close to the dead timber. Brownlin was with him until Brownlin got shot in the leg.''

''Rolf, think about the end of this,'' Kyle continued.

"Simeon is already in big trouble with the law, and you're now a party to contributing to this war by not going to Julian first. Help me to send the farmers home. Julian could be a lot more understanding with Simeon if you help keep the peace."

Rolf considered Kyle's words thoughtfully. "There is no question to the wisdom of what you say, and I won't argue with you, but you cannot handle Jory and Bolden by yourself."

"I don't want anyone else shot. How's the cowboy who was already taken?"

"He's with Brownlin. But he wasn't wounded, just caught," Rolf answered. "Come on, there's cover to where Brownlin is keeping him."

By the time Kyle and Rolf had gained Brownlin's position, the swollen storm clouds had cast a gray veil over the land. Raindrops pelleted sporadically, and the constant boom of thunder crept closer. Kyle saw that Brownlin had lost a lot of blood, and his face showed the strain of his vigilance over his prisoner, but Brownlin wasn't the only one glad to see them.

"Rivers! Doggone, am I tickled to see you!" the cowboy cried.

"Why is that?" Kyle inquired.

"We were trying to slip out of Queenie's outfit, but before we could get off this cussed mountain, these farmers opened fire on us."

"Did you boys take a hand in destroying Jory Breene's place?"

"Bolden ordered us to tear out his taters and fences. I reckon we're guilty of that, but we didn't know there was gonna be any fire put to anything and neither did Bolden. He and Queenie had an awful fight over that, but while they were fighting, us boys decided that that woman was as crazy-mean as a pig-eyed horse and we've done had enough. We'll work for Bolden but not for her." He paused for a moment, studying the two farmers. "We didn't want a fight with you farmers, and we wouldn't have shot back today if that hotheaded varmint hadn't started throwing lead in our faces. Rivers, I swear we were leaving!"

"Who's fighting the farmers, then?" Kyle asked.

"Bolden is, for a reason, but as for Queenie, she's just out to raise the devil!"

"What's Bolden's reason?"

"He hates that barbed wire they string up around those fields. It cuts the cows all to pieces, and he had to shoot his favorite horse 'cause it cut one of its legs almost completely off. Bolden hates wire and therefore he wants the farmers out of this valley, but he ain't behind trying to kill people and burn their homes. That's Queenie's game."

"But he hired a professional killer," Kyle said. "That's being in favor of killing."

The cowboy stared at Kyle, then at the farmers, then back at Kyle. "*You're* a hired killer," he whispered hesitantly, not sure whether to put it to Kyle's face.

"Who told you that?" Kyle demanded.

"Queenie said you was."

"Well, the lady is plumb loco!" Kyle answered hotly.

"That's for sure, but that's why Bolden hired the gun . . . I mean, that's why he agreed to hire him. Queenie's the one that squalled until he finally gave in, but Bolden agreed only because he himself won't fool with a fast gun like you. And since we all thought that the farmers hired you, it seemed kinda right, as we saw it. But now . . . well, if you wasn't hired, I reckon it was all wrong."

Kyle took a tally of the farmers he could see hidden near the downed timber. Jory Breene crouched under a fallen log beneath the cowboy's commanding cover, attempting to get closer without being seen.

"Can you get your pards to hold their fire?" Kyle questioned.

"I think so," the cowboy said. "We wasn't wanting a battle when we got this one."

Kyle looked at Rolf. "Can you get your hands on Jory and bring him down here?" After Rolf's nod, Kyle looked at the cowboy and indicated the deadfall. "Get things cooled so Rolf don't get shot."

The cowboy removed his hat and waved it in the air as he stood up slowly. Then he cupped his hands and hollered up toward the pile of deadfall:

"Shorty! Buckles! You boys up there hold your fire! We got the law here!" Several hats waved back at them, and then the cowboy nodded at Kyle. "That's as good as their word. They won't shoot unless they get shot at again.''

Suddenly a bolt of lightning struck nearby, and hissing pops peppered the air with the smell of sulfur. The deafening, earthshaking explosion that followed the blinding flash seemed to rip open the heavens, and torrents of hail blanketed the ground and cascaded from the cliffs above.

Rolf didn't wait for Kyle's orders. He laid his rifle beneath a rock and stepped out from his cover, bowing against the storm as he worked his way toward Jory Breene. However, the hot-tempered man saw him coming, and apparently had guessed from the hollered words that the fracas was about to end. Rolf was out to stop him and that was a thing that Jory didn't intend to let happen.

Kyle moved from the protection of the rocks and out into the open, watching Rolf pursue Jory up the boulder-strewn slope. Suddenly Jory became cornered and Rolf closed in on him. There was no visible contest, but Kyle could see it wasn't because Jory didn't want to fight Rolf. It was because he was helpless, snugly tucked in under Rolf's arm like a bulging bedroll. The hail changed to heavy rain as Rolf began picking his way back down the treacherous rock slope with Jory pinned securely in the crook of his arm.

Abruptly Rolf stopped his descent and pointed his free arm up the draw to behind Kyle. He yelled something that Kyle couldn't hear, but Kyle did understand the urgency in Rolf's tone. He spun in his tracks and his eyes came to level on Bolden's hired gun, who was not more than a hundred feet from him. The rain poured off the man's hat and ran down his long coat.

"Rivers! You're dead!" the man yelled above the storm, whipping back his long-tailed coat.

There was no hesitation, no tense moments before the draw, and no words wasted. The gunfighter reached for his pistol in the same motion of throwing back his coat, but that action was clearly read by Kyle Rivers. As if each man were the shimmering reflection of the other on the surface of a quiet pool, together they drew and together they fired.

Another blinding flash and a sharp crack accompanied the explosion of the revolvers as Kyle was spun halfway around and slammed against a monstrous rock by the impact of lead. He fell to his knees and twisted as he raised his gun to fire back up the draw. He halted there, frozen in his actions as his eyes squinted through the drenching rain at the gunman sprawled facedown against the earth.

Kyle sank to the ground and leaned his back against the rock, staring through the rain to where death leered back at him. After a moment he forced his eyes away from it and examined the burning wound in his left shoulder. The gunman hadn't missed by much. A few more inches to the left and Kyle would have joined the man lying in the cold rain. He looked up as Rolf came puffing toward him with Jory in hand.

"Thank God!" Rolf sighed. "I saw you go down, and I figured Rube was gonna get to use his box. How bad are you?"

"I'm not dead, and I reckon that's all that matters."

Kyle grunted as he got to his feet and holstered the .45. Rolf and Jory accompanied him to where the gunfighter lay in the mud. He knelt and started to roll the man over, but he saw a hole in the coat just over the left shoulder and didn't need to go any further.

He rose and looked up the draw and then toward the deadfall where the cowboys stood on the edge of the slope and looked down at them. Kyle motioned them down, watching Jory Breene as he did so.

"I reckon you got a gripe," Kyle told him. And then his gray eyes turned threatening. "But you take it to Julian and leave it in his hands. Cowboy or farmer, the next man that disobeys me today will risk a chance of following hot on this killer's heels." He quickly put his attention on Rolf. "You and Jory get Brownlin to the doc's and turn Tritch loose when you get down there." Kyle handed Rolf the key to the handcuffs.

"Where are *you* going?" Rolf asked.

"Bolden and Queenie haven't showed, so I figure they must be in the cut with the hidden horses," Kyle answered.

The cowboy that Brownlin had been keeping at gunpoint suddenly joined the group. He studied the man on the ground, then pointed up the ravine. "Bolden and Queenie are with the horses. He's got a reason to be in the fight, but she's the one I'd watch if I were you. I reckon the boys will give you a hand and tag along. Besides, our horses are up there.''

Kyle shook his head. "No, Bolden and Queenie had to see this, and I doubt Bolden is dumb enough to start any personal gunplay against the law. He sent out his ace in the hole. You boys just sit snug.''

The downpour continued, drenching the already boggy ground still further, and making it difficult to walk up the ravine. Kyle had to watch his footing. Edging around a boulder, he got a full view of the horses huddled together and, in their midst, a woman with her back to him as she quickly pulled up a cinch and swung aboard.

At that moment, Kyle was trying to locate Bolden, but when the woman turned the horse toward him, Kyle saw her face and the inner jolt of it chased caution from his mind.

"Betsy!" he blurted out hoarsely, stunned momentarily by the surprise of it all. Abruptly he recovered and reached for the gun on his hip as she spurred the horse toward him. She jerked the horse to a stop when his gun came to level, and she stared him in the eye, unblinking against the stinging rain.

"Betsy," he said again, but this time his voice was cold and threatening. "Time to pay up."

"Not yet, Rivers," Bolden hissed uncomfortably close to his ear as he crammed a cold barrel against Kyle's skull. "Drop it. And, mister, this day I don't need a reason!"

Kyle let the gun slide from his fingers, and it hit the mud with a splat. Bolden had the drop on him again.

Queenie edged her horse closer. A cold beauty graced her features, and nature had favored her figure, but her eyes threatened and belittled from their greenish depths. She started to dismount, but hesitated warily, keeping her distance from Kyle. Suddenly, something else seemed to come to birth in Kyle's mind, and he saw a hollow cavity behind her eyes, a selfish strife that gnawed away at that first impression of her prettiness.

"Were you going to kill me, Kyle?" she purred, first smirking, then letting a hateful, snarling look cross her face.

There was nothing there in front of him, nothing at all. What had been the woman he had loved and married, and then had nursed a burning hate for, hadn't been worth those years of torment. In that moment, he saw it all for the waste that it was. He almost felt a gratefulness toward Bolden for ramming the gun against his head. Otherwise, in his first raging burn of temper, the ending here might have been decidedly different for the monstrous and pathetic creature who looked down at him from the horse's back.

"You owe me an answer," Kyle said quietly.

"Answer?" she snapped, "The answer is wealth. Look around you, Kyle. This is my land. I'm rich . . . are you? Have you seen my home? It's a mansion. Where is *your* home—under a sagebrush? No, Kyle,

Jeb wasn't the man you are. I'll give you that. But Jeb had what you'd never have. You were content to be a poor cowboy, content with love and raising a family of brats. I was destined for better things than that. But I'd never get there with you in the way. You should be thankful that I didn't have you killed instead of put away! Now you leave me no choice. Bolden, take care of him!''

"Don't flatter yourself, woman," Kyle whipped out quickly. "I didn't come here because I care about you."

"You don't?" she whispered in bewilderment.

"Where is my child?"

Kyle felt the barrel of the gun let up, then altogether leave the back of his head. He held his breath and waited. But nothing happened. Then Bolden spoke:

"Was this the man you were married to when you met Jeb?"

"So what if I was? I said take care of him!"

When Bolden spoke again, his tone sounded strange: "Answer him, Betsy."

"Where's my child?" Kyle demanded again, unable to control the hope in his voice, the hope that had given him strength through the years to continue his search.

She glared at him. Then she threw back her head and laughed in faked boisterousness. She sobered and wrinkled her face in disdain.

"Child? You mean that miserable thing you cursed upon me? Is that what brings you here? You've wasted your time, darling," she said, making the word "darling" sound like some kind of pity. "The child died at birth."

Kyle shuddered. He breathed deep and fought for his bearings, because he seemed to be nowhere, groping at something beyond his reach. A protective numbness brought him back to the rain and the ravine and the two people near him. The tiredness he had felt at the grave was nothing compared to what descended upon him at that moment.

"My, did that bother you, Kyle?" she taunted.

Bolden stepped around to the front and looked Kyle in the face. Upon the rancher's face burned an emotion that Kyle couldn't read, but it wasn't threatening. Bolden reached down and picked up the muddy gun. Bolden studied the weapon a moment, then slipped it back into Kyle's holster. He kept his own gun leveled at Kyle's chest, holding the hammer back with his thumb.

"I reckon that if I was you, I wouldn't try to use that unless you want it to blow up in your face. The barrel's full of mud." Bolden backed away, keeping his attention on both Kyle and Betsy. "We're riding out, so don't be a fool. Like I said, today I'll shoot you for blinking."

"Riding out?" Betsy echoed, then piled out of the saddle and faced Bolden, taking on a stance that reminded Kyle of a hissing cat on the fight. "He's gunning for the farmers. You're the fool! I said kill him!" She stormed and stomped her feet like she'd stepped in a pile of ants. "How dare you disobey me! I'll have you run off this place!"

Bolden showed no expression as he studied her. Then he turned to Kyle again. "Get over against the rocks."

"Was it a son?" Kyle asked.

Betsy laughed again. "No, it was a girl," she said, smirking.

"Rivers, I said get over there against the rocks and out of our way. I ain't gonna tell you again." Bolden shot a look at his wife. "Mount up. We're getting out of here," he ordered, but there was a strange look in his eyes and his voice carried a dangerous tone to it.

Kyle now had all the answers, and those answers were all the wrong ones. He obeyed Bolden in shocked numbness, yet the numbness helped him to handle the loss. Moments later, he stood in the blasting sheets of rain and watched Bolden's and Queenie's horses labor through the splashing mud and disappear in the foggy gray mist.

Chapter Nine

THROUGH the blurriness of the deluge, the forms
of the cowboys came toward Kyle, but he gazed
on past the men and into the dankness where Bolden
and Queenie had disappeared.

"What happened, Rivers? Are you hurt?" one of
them asked.

"A little," Kyle muttered. Then he forced himself
to deal with the business at hand. "I reckon you better
tell Julian your side of this deal that you boys pulled
against Jory Breene."

"We've already discussed it and agreed to do that
very thing," the cowboy said. "Are you sure you're
all right? You got blood running down your arm."

Kyle glanced at the wound in his shoulder, but the
aching burn was nothing compared to what staggered
him from within.

"Yeah, I'm all right," he answered, and walked away down the incline to where his horse was tied.

The ending of day cast an even deeper gloominess into the downpour. Kyle mounted wearily and nudged the black onto the trail. Then he changed his mind and put the horse back into the brush. He allowed the reins to slop, and the horse picked a direction and plodded slowly through the puddles, splashing mud and water as it drifted with the storm.

Kyle felt lost, like a ship without a sail, in a storm of life that had no sunlight ahead. He was aware that darkness had settled in, yet he let the horse meander with the storm.

There was no revenge to this ending; nothing sweet, nothing bitter. Revenge was like the pot of gold at the end of the rainbow, promising all the world, pulling a man onward. But in the end, the reward was nothing.

The horse wandered on into the soggy night, and though he was thoroughly soaked, the hours in the cold rain seemed to cleanse something in Kyle's soul that had rotted for a long while. Late in the night, he turned the horse sideways to the wind and headed back toward Cedar Point. Hours later, the black halted of its own accord and Kyle recognized the river that flowed east of the schoolhouse, and he realized that he had come too far west to make connections with the town. Then Karen came to mind, and her image seemed to beckon to him. He nudged the horse across the river and urged it onward.

He could barely make out the building in the middle of the small clearing as he rode up in the driving torrent. The thunder raged and lightning cracked so close that it made him cringe. He tied the horse and made his way toward the extension at the back of the schoolhouse. He knocked, leaning tiredly against the doorjamb. The flare from a bolt of lightning lit up the door, and then the boom shook the building. He knocked again, louder.

"Who's there?" Karen asked in a firm voice.

"Kyle Rivers," he said.

It was quiet; then her voice came from just inside the door. "Mr. Rivers, what do you want?"

"Let me in."

"But it's night and—"

"And it's raining and thundering," he muttered, leaning his head against the door, somehow unable to explain from outside what had brought him.

He heard the bar lift, and then the door opened. Karen stood there for a moment before she stepped back.

"Come in, Mr. Rivers."

He stepped in out of the storm into the dark interior. He felt for the door and shut it behind him. Then he reached for her and pulled her against him. She gasped and cried, "Mr. Rivers, you're wet and cold. Let me go!"

Kyle knew that what he was doing was wrong. He released her and leaned back against the door, wondering why it had ever crossed his mind that she would welcome him wet and cold in the middle of the night.

He grasped the door, pulled it open, walked back out into the rain, and closed the door behind him. Before he could take another step, the door opened.

"Kyle, come back in here!"

Yesterday he would have kept on walking. Tonight, well, tonight he would obey her. He went back inside and closed the door again. They stood silently in the darkness. When he reached out for her, she allowed it.

"What's wrong, Kyle?" she asked.

"Hold me," he murmured as he closed his arms around her.

Kyle held her gently to him in the darkness that was occasionally lit up by lightning through the cabin's tiny windows. He couldn't stop holding her, and the time went by, but she didn't struggle with him about being rudely soaked in the middle of the night. He trembled with the fatigue of his emptiness.

"I came to Cedar Point following a man . . . to kill him," he began, answering the need to get out his rage and thus rid himself of it. "I came here following a woman—to do what to her, I didn't know. But I believed there was a child, a son . . . my own son. Karen, I wanted that boy more than anything on this earth. I dreamed it—I lived it."

A great pain tore at him, causing him to clutch her more strongly to him. He lowered his head and rested his face against her cheek. Then more words came to him.

"I was married to Betsy Bolden. There was a child, but she died. I didn't know about it until today, and why it's more than I can handle I don't know, but I can't. The end of this is too empty, just too cussed empty!"

He held her silently for a long while after that, but the worst had passed, and he was able to get a grip on himself. He had been there for her that day in the hayloft when Mrs. Brown had been shot, and tonight she had been there for him.

"Thanks, Karen," he murmured, and he kissed her lightly.

"How about some coffee now?"

He nodded and released her. She lit the lantern and set it on a small table. He looked around and immediately noticed the neatness of the tiny room where kitchen, bedroom, and parlor were all one. She pointed to a chair, and he seated himself as she put on the coffee and stoked up the stove until the fire crackled and snapped. She came and sat down across the table from him, but immediately sprang to her feet.

"You're hurt!" she exclaimed, starting around the table.

"I've been hit, but the wound is clean."

"I'll put on some water and—"

"No. It will hold until I get to town. Don't fuss over me, Karen."

She eased back into her chair, but her eyes showed concern as she continued to study the hole in his shirt.

"When you came to Cedar Point, you said that you were looking and then you'd move on," she said, searching his eyes. "Will you stay now that your search is over?"

"No," he answered quietly.

"It's going to destroy Danny Brown when you go."

"Yeah, that bothers me. I don't know what to do about what I've started there, but I've got several more weeks of sentence to work out, so I'll be here long enough to break it to him easy. Maybe, in the meantime, I can find the family that the boy needs."

"It's you he needs, Kyle. He's not your flesh and blood, but he needs you."

He pondered for a few moments, then shook his head. "No, Karen, he can't go with me. Julian said something today and he's right. I've learned to live with this gun on my hip, and I know it'll stay there. That wouldn't be a life to drag a boy through."

"I didn't want you to take him with you," she said. "I thought that was perhaps reason enough for you to stay. Would you have dragged your own son around the country if you had found him?"

"I didn't find him." He looked at her sharply. "But that part of my life is gone, and I don't want to talk about it."

When the coffee was ready, she poured a cup for each of them and sat down again. There was something else on her mind, and Kyle realized that when she sipped her cup but wouldn't look at him.

"What is it, teacher?"

"Was Betsy the only woman you could love?"

As his eyes traveled over her face, a gentle grin replaced the bitter grimace that had dominated his features for hours. He took a drink and set down the cup, totally aware of the meaning behind her question.

"I thought you loved boys of school age," he said.

"I do . . . but Kyle, I . . . well, you are hard not to think about," she finished in a whisper.

He silently watched her, waiting for her to look at him. When she did, he could see the red hue on her cheeks, even in the dim lantern light.

"I shouldn't have uttered such a thing," she said hushedly.

"No, not when you're so against being kissed that you'd sign a contract that prohibits it."

"That wasn't why I signed that. It was required and teaching comes first. It's my life, Kyle."

Karen got up from her chair and went to the stove. She vigorously shoved in several chunks of kindling. Then she took a deep breath and turned around.

"I love children and I love teaching. But I also . . . oh, Kyle, you mustn't act like you had only one chance in life. If your dream has ended, then begin another!"

"You also—what?" he bantered.

"You know very well my meaning."

"I think so, but I'd like to hear it," he said.

Karen looked as if she were going to speak, but, instead, she pursed her lips, seated herself gracefully, and folded her hands on her lap. There was no haughtiness in her manner, but when she lifted her chin, Kyle was struck with the realization of how dignified a lady she was.

"Mr. Rivers, I believe any further steps along that line should come from you, the man."

He looked at her intently, but maintained his silence as he continued to drink from his cup. He drained it, then rose to his feet, still looking at her.

Karen bent her head slightly and gazed at her folded hands. "I guess," she said, "that your silence means I just made a fool of myself."

"My silence is something you shouldn't guess at," he said softly, and walked to the door. "By the way," he said, looking over his shoulder at her, "I could never have loved Betsy as much as I could love you. But I will be riding on."

"Why?" she asked.

"Tonight I have buried a part of me with that dream. Before I can begin another dream, I think, perhaps, there must be time and maybe miles. But maybe not. I really don't know. But I do know that if I responded to your words tonight, it would be an injustice to the truth of things."

They exchanged somber looks. Then Karen suddenly found a smile. "You're sentenced to church again tomorrow."

"Yes, ma'am."

"Would Danny like me to . . ." she asked wistfully.

"I haven't asked Danny," he said, "but *I* would like your company, Karen."

She beamed like the morning sun, and her smile seemed to take the chill out of the wind that whipped through the open doorway. "Thank you. I'll be in town by nine."

"No, ma'am, I'll pick you up by nine. Good night."

The rain was over, but the wind continued, breezing lightly, but causing Kyle to shiver as he rode toward Cedar Point. Instead of dwelling on his loss, his thoughts settled on Karen McLaughlin. By the time he rode into town, the glowing promise of another day prodded at the horizon. He stabled his horse, went down the walk, and turned in at the doctor's office.

After his wound was treated, he entered Julian's office. Julian was seated in his chair, looking like he hadn't slept a wink. His lips attempted a grin but failed, so he removed the pipe stem from between them and the grin matured.

"I see the badge didn't burn a hole in your hide," he taunted gently. Then his face became serious. "I've worried all night about what happened to you. I was never so relieved to see a man walk through that door." He studied Kyle. "Thanks. I don't know how else to say it." His expression turned a little foxy, and he added, "Of course, I could put you on the payroll."

Kyle reached up and curled his fingers around the

badge. He slowly removed it from his shirt and laid it on the desk in front of Julian. Then he eased down in a chair and said quietly, "I'll be moving on as soon as I finish out my sentence."

Julian frowned. "This office was packed with people last night. Cowboys and farmers stood next to one another, talking sense, coming up with solutions. The cowboys are gonna build Jory a new barn and a house too. Jory wouldn't stand for them to get near his spud patch, so they don't have to plant taters, but they've got to build a fence."

Julian took a deep breath and picked up the badge. He fingered it and went on without looking at Kyle.

"The farmers told how you managed to send them all home without drawing your iron. Every danged one of them, farmer and cowboy, must have told me twice how you beat that hired gun to the draw. They all knew you could have gunned the situation to a sliding stop up there on the mountain, but, no, you talked the men out of a war without spilling one ounce of community blood. Men who could have done that are few and far between, especially if they had the ability with a gun that you have."

Julian laid the badge down on the desk and looked across to Kyle's steady eyes.

"I told them I'd asked you to take the job here with me. They whooped and hollered, and Schweeney said that as far as he was concerned, you didn't owe him any more work, so you could take the job immediately.

The preacher wouldn't budge, and therefore that sentence is still in force. What I'm saying, Rivers, is that there's a place here for you. Now, doggone it, take it!''

"No, Julian.''

"Would it make a difference if I told you that Karen can see the sun rise and set in you?''

"No.''

"Why not?''

"I reckon she has a dream.''

"Kyle Rivers, if you ain't smart enough to see that teaching fell by the wayside the day you rode into town, then I'll tell you outright that she had to confide in somebody and that somebody is me. I ain't mouthing off—I'm telling you the gospel truth!''

"I won't stay in this town any longer than I have to,'' Kyle answered.

"Give me one blasted reason why!'' Julian demanded.

"Queenie Bolden was my wife, and I reckon that living in the same town with her would be a little unpleasant.''

Julian stared at Kyle, then slowly put his pipe between his teeth and leaned back in his chair. "And Jeb Grosse was Bolden's stepson,'' he said, nodding. "So, I should have guessed that she was the other person you were looking for, since Jeb showed up with her after he'd been off roaming around.''

"I'm surprised you didn't guess it.''

"You wanted her back?"

"Nope. I wanted my child, but that was only a dream that I had no proof about, and as it turned out, doggin' this trail has all been a waste of effort. You know, Julian, a man who thinks he can live for revenge is stealing his own life. I'm glad it's over." Kyle got to his feet.

"You're just gonna walk out on Danny Brown?" Julian asked, grasping for anything that might keep Kyle in Cedar Point.

"Good day, Sheriff. I'll see you in church."

Julian's last remark caused Kyle to head for the livery and look for Danny. He found the boy brushing the black. Danny turned and looked long at Kyle, then went back to his job.

"I reckon I was scared when you didn't come in with the rest of them," Danny mumbled, his use of the word "reckon" evidence of how he copied everything he could about Kyle.

"Reckon I needed a night ride," Kyle answered.

"I wish I could ride with you sometime, Mr. Rivers," Danny said quietly.

Kyle watched the boy while he worked. Then an idea came into his mind and he strode over to Julian's saddled horse. He led the gentle beast from the stall, and as Danny turned to watch, he motioned to the boy and said, "Untie my horse and bring it over here. Then climb up on the sheriff's horse, son. We're gonna go for a ride."

Danny trembled. Then he took several gulps that helped the happiness in his eyes to keep from turning into happy tears. His mouth quivered at the corners as he stared at Kyle. Then he rushed to the manger, untied the black, and handed the halter rope to Kyle.

Kyle understood how the word "son" had affected the orphan, because he knew that the word "dad" would surely affect him the same way. Suddenly, as if reading from a book that had been open and in front of him all this time, he understood. Danny wasn't of his own blood, but he was every bit the son that he had dreamed about. As he lifted the youngster up on the horse's back, he let his hand linger on Danny for a moment.

"Do you mind me calling you son, Danny?"

"Aw, Mr. Rivers," Danny said, his mouth quivering again, "it's even better than being called pardner."

Kyle grinned and playfully poked Danny a light blow to the chest. Danny grinned and let fly with a wild but mimicking punch at Kyle's arm. Kyle moved in next to his black, and as he swung onto its back and gathered up the halter rope, he looked at Danny in playful sternness.

"We're gonna have to work on your swing, son."

As they rode down the street, Kyle saw Julian sitting on a chair on the boardwalk just outside his office. The lawman straightened, then nodded approvingly without taking his pipe from his mouth. Kyle guided the black that way, and said lightly as they passed, "Temporary horse theft. We'll be back in about an hour."

During the first half hour of that ride, Kyle Rivers made up his mind. As far as he was concerned, he had found his son.

Kyle had promised to pick Karen up around nine o'clock, and he was beginning to be pressed for time. Once he had made up his mind, there were two more things he needed to do. He left Danny at the livery with instructions to be on time for church, and then he headed back to Julian's office.

"Heck, you didn't have to come tell me you were back, Rivers. I'd have given you all the time you wanted with my horse this morning."

"Does that steady job pay enough to feed a family?"

Julian's eyes opened in disbelief. Then his hand trembled as it opened the desk drawer and brought out the badge.

"It does if the deputy wears the badge on the outside."

Kyle reached down and took the badge from Julian. After pinning it on his shirt with a grin, he nodded and said, "I'll take the job."

Kyle went to the door and turned the knob, intending to get the buggy from the livery and drive out to the schoolhouse, but he pulled Reuben Sparks into the room with the door when he jerked it inward.

Rube sputtered, "Do you have to manhandle everything?" The undertaker strode over to Julian, but glared back over his shoulder at Kyle. "I reckon you're tickled I never could find a box to fit your carcass, Rivers. And I'll add that I hope I never do." Rube put both hands on Julian's desk and leaned toward the lawman. "I just found a box to fit Queenie Bolden. She was lyin' dead out by the bridge east of town. Shot in the chest. And it looks like she tried to make it to the doc's but lost the race. I left her down at the bridge so you can investigate if you want."

Kyle recoiled as if he were hit in the face. Recovering, he saw Julian looking hard at him, and he looked at Julian right back.

"Don't speak what you're thinking, my friend," Kyle warned Julian.

"If you think I'm pointing a finger at you, you're wrong," Julian growled. "I'm thinking that Bolden has been a prime suspect concerning Mrs. Brown, and now the queen comes up dead too. What I'm thinking is that there were only two men I know of that might have had reason to kill Queenie Bolden, and both of them were out in that storm. One of them was you and the other was Bolden, who didn't come into town with the men. It looks like I've got a woman-killer on my hands, and this first job of yours ain't gonna be easy. Go after Bolden, right now. And I'm leaving it to your judgment Kyle. Do whatever you have to, but I'd prefer you to bring him in."

"Can I use your horse? Mine needs a rest."

"Sure," Julian answered. But his character wouldn't

allow him not to badger Kyle a little in spite of the circumstances. "But don't you use this as an excuse to duck out on church this morning. You get back here as quick as you can."

"Sheriff, I wouldn't miss church this morning for anything in the world. Would you have Jory or Brownlin go out and pick up Karen McLaughlin for me?"

Chapter Ten

T HE morning sun had a good start on its climb up the sky when Kyle rode through the gate to Bolden's spread. He allowed the horse to walk, carefully checking out the places that might hide a man. As he neared the house, he reined his horse at the side of it instead of tying it to the rack in front.

On foot, he eased around the corner of the huge, two-story structure and listened. Then he vaulted over the railing on the covered porch and walked softly to the front door. He tried the handle and it turned. He let the elaborately carved oak door swing in by itself, and then he entered and quickly slid against the wall.

What met his eyes was enough wealth to take away most people's breath, but Kyle had no use for wealth. The expensive furnishings told of success, but they also emitted an air of coldness that almost made him shudder. His footsteps were soundless as he crossed an intricately woven rug and peered cautiously into a room beyond an archway.

The far wall in the room seemed more than fifty feet away and two cavernous fireplaces yawned back into it. In the middle of the area, several high-backed lazy chairs faced the fireplaces. Bolden sat in one of them, and he was looking up at a large painting of the queen herself. The rancher seemed deep in thought, and the covered floors allowed Kyle to walk up behind him without making a sound.

He pulled the .45 and laid the bore in the curve of Bolden's ear. The man twitched and went rigid, but he didn't turn his head.

"Let me guess," Bolden said softly. "Kyle Rivers has the drop on me this time."

"I see you're packing iron, so take it out easy and lay it on the floor," Kyle ordered.

"You ain't got reason for this," Bolden protested, but he placed his gun on the floor beside the chair.

"I'm afraid I have."

"Name it."

"The queen put to rest?"

When Bolden started to turn his head, Kyle butted him lightly with the bore of his .45.

"So, she didn't make it," Bolden whispered.

"I'm here to arrest you for that."

Bolden took a deep breath. Then he looked up at the painting again. "Are you telling me the truth, Rivers? Is she gone?"

"Reckon she's with Reuben Sparks right now."

"Well, I can defend myself as far as Betsy's concerned, but it's time for things to be said that I'd never have told while she was alive."

"You can tell Julian," Kyle said.

"No. Most of this is for your ears, Rivers."

"And Widow Brown—can you defend yourself on that one?"

The rancher immediately reddened in the face, and he began to tremble. This time Kyle allowed Bolden to turn his head and look at him.

"I ain't that kind of man," he growled. "And if you wasn't holding that iron, I'd beat you senseless for accusing me of it!"

"Did you shoot Betsy?"

"Yes and no," Bolden answered, continuing to look at Kyle with steady eyes. "But I was square with you up there in that ravine, and I let you have your little chat with her when I could have dropped you in the mud. You've called me wrong here today, so give me enough rope to have my say."

Kyle pondered a few moments, and then he nudged the rancher in the back. "Get up and walk toward the fireplace." After a good distance separated them, Kyle stopped him. "Now turn and sit cross-legged on the floor." As soon as Bolden had complied, Kyle eased down in the chair and slid his .45 into its holster. Then he picked up Bolden's weapon and checked the cylinder. Kyle laid the loaded pistol idly across his knee.

"I'm listening, Bolden," he said, leaning back as he watched the man warily.

It took Bolden a moment to gather his thoughts. "It's hard enough for a marriage without the difference of years. Betsy and I started out with greed as a basis for our marriage. Then this old fool here fell in love. She never did with me, though, but I still loved her." Bolden struggled for a minute, then went on.

"I guess, to make it short, we had some bad words after we left you yesterday. I told her it'd be a cold day when she ran me off this spread, and that really made her hiss and snarl. She informed me that she already had me in hot water, and that's when I found out that she'd ridden my horse and taken a shot at Rolf. She did that to get the law on my tail so I'd have to make a run for my life and she'd end up with the ranch all to herself. She actually tried to kill Rolf, but thank God she missed. That's why you were looking at my sorrel's shoes, wasn't it, Rivers?"

Kyle nodded.

Bolden went on: "I called her some low-down names and let her know that the day before Jeb died, he told me about the rotten stunts they'd pulled on you, and that she wouldn't get away with pulling them on me. Jeb was my stepson if you don't already know that. Well, Betsy came uncorked when I told her I knew all about things. Then she went on to enlighten me on subjects no man could accept, no matter how much he loved a woman. The longer she ranted, the more plain it became that the only important thing in her life was the power to control men. She drove me and she drove Jeb, but she couldn't drive you, and that ate at her. I found out that she took shells out of your saddlebags and planted them at Widow Brown's cabin. She even used your horse in the middle of the night to do it. Then she took a shot at you the night Julian put you in jail."

Bolden took several deep breaths and looked up at the high ceiling. Then he again put his steady eyes on Kyle.

"That was when I asked her how she knew to plant shells that night at the widow's house. But as soon as I asked it, I knew the answer. I just shut up and stared at her. I finally said, 'You murdered that old woman.' I tell you, Rivers, for years I had trouble accepting the fact that she let her baby die. In the end, I forced myself to accept it because I loved her. But murdering an old lady merely for the sake of controlling you, Rivers, was something I couldn't accept. It turned me cold. I pulled my gun and told her we were going to the sheriff, and that's when she leaped at me and we got in a wrestle with the gun and it went off. I'm telling you straight: I couldn't pull a trigger on a woman, not even someone as loco as Betsy. That incident lies somewhere between an accident and defending myself against her temper."

"Why didn't you help her get to the doctor after the gun went off?" Kyle asked.

"I tried, but when I dropped the gun and grabbed

her, she got her hands on it and barely missed killing me. That was when I quit. Love has its limits, and it had turned cold inside of me. I just plain quit her. I dodged out the door and saddled my horse. Then I took a ride in the rain and left her to whatever. I never looked back. She was gone this morning when I came home.''

''Is that it, Bolden?'' Kyle inquired coolly.

''That's what happened and why. I shot her, I guess, but I don't deserve to have to pay for it.''

''What about what you've done to the farmers?''

''I wanted them out, and I admit I tried every way I knew how. But I never shot anybody and I wasn't a party to burning Jory's house and barn.''

''So, what do you think you do deserve to pay for?''

''I don't deserve to pay for a murder I didn't really commit. Otherwise, I'm content to take whatever punishment Julian's law comes up with concerning the farmers.''

Kyle studied Bolden intently. ''I reckon somebody might believe all that, but there's no reason at all that killing Mrs. Brown would give Betsy any kind of control over me. That's the hole in your tale, Bolden, because I never even knew Widow Brown.''

''It ain't a hole, Rivers. The argument got started yesterday because I cussed Betsy for lying to you about the baby being a girl. All these years I thought that baby had died. Then I found out last night that it didn't. Betsy couldn't kill her own child, no matter how rotten she was to the rest of the world. Mrs. Brown is the only one that knew, and Betsy had to keep that last secret from you. You see Rivers, Danny Brown is your son!''

This time Kyle knew the truth when he heard it. He was full of a feeling that could match the magnitude of the color in the sunset, and the joyful thankfulness that ran rampant inside him caused him to tremble outwardly.

''I'm a man without children,'' Bolden continued somberly, nodding at what he saw had overcome Kyle. ''I wouldn't keep such a secret from another man.''

Kyle got to his feet and motioned to Bolden to stand up. ''Anything more you want to say before you talk to Julian?'' Bolden shook his head. ''Then you bring yourself in as soon as you can get there. If I have to come looking for you, I *will* find you!''

Bolden lifted his brows in surprise, then he nodded and a faint smile crossed his lips. ''I'll be there. Go on, get back to that boy before you explode.''

Church services were well under way when Kyle cantered into town. Julian had stayed at the jail, waiting for Kyle to return with the rancher, and as Kyle dismounted in front of his office, Julian frowned from the doorway.

''Doggone it, Rivers, I was hoping you didn't have to shoot him.''

''I didn't.''

"Then why didn't you bring him in?"

"I reckon things ain't what they looked, so I told him to bring himself in."

"And what if he just told you a cock-and-bull story so he could skip out?"

Kyle saw a rider coming down the road far east of town. It was Bolden's sorrel. He turned back to Julian. "I reckon it was just a real strong feeling before, but now I see the proof. Why don't you ask Bolden for the answers when he gets here?" Kyle indicated the oncoming rider as he grinned at Julian. "You said to use my judgement, and Julian, my judgment is that I believe him. Excuse me now, but I'm missing out on my sermon."

He walked briskly to the church and entered quietly, soon locating Karen and Danny near the front. He eased down next to Danny, and his somberness caused the boy's broad smile to disappear. Kyle's deep feelings were not the kind that he would show in public. Immediately he averted his eyes and studied Karen.

The preacher talked on, but Kyle didn't hear any of it. Karen met his eyes once, and saw something so strong within him gazing back at her that she blushed and put her attention on the sermon. Kyle slid an arm round Danny's shoulders and gave him a firm clench. Then he extended his hand and brushed Karen across the cheek with a finger. Her blush intensified and she quickly gave him a look that said to behave himself. He did it again.

The pump organ came to her rescue as the sermon ended and people stood up to sing a hymn. Danny continued to stare up at Kyle, well aware that his partner had something awfully strong on his mind.

As the closing prayer drifted over the congregation, Kyle slyly traded places with Danny and clasped one hand over Karen's folded ones. She looked at him sharply, then the realization of what she saw in his eyes took her mind off setting an example as the community teacher.

"Oh, Kyle," she whispered, and leaned her head against his shoulder. He tightened his grip on her hands, and put an arm round her and held her until the prayer ended.

As the organ began again and the preacher headed toward the front door to shake people's hands as they left, Kyle reached down and grabbed Danny by one hand and Karen by the other. The people around them should have been leaving, but, instead, were staring at them.

"Side door, Karen," Kyle muttered.

Only seconds later they left the church and stood in the noonday sun. Kyle didn't stop. He led them around the back into the shade of several cottonwoods, and there let go of their hands and dropped to one knee in front of Danny. He put his hands on the boy's shoulders and barely stifled the emotion inside of himself as he looked into Danny's eyes and said:

"You aren't an orphan of any kind. I came to this

town searching for my son, who was once stolen from me. I have searched for years, and today I found the man who knew about you. Danny, you're my own son, my real son, my own—''

Emotion overcame Kyle, and he wrapped his arms around Danny and hugged him desperately. Danny's arms couldn't reach around Kyle, but they tried for all they were worth. When Kyle finally released him, Danny couldn't hold back his tears, but he wiped them with the back of his hand, causing a smudge across his freckled cheek.

''My real, live dad?'' the boy whispered through trembling lips.

''Your real dad.''

''Forever?''

''Forever,'' Kyle repeated.

Danny slowly reached out and touched Kyle's shirt with his stubby fingers. Then, with his eyes devouring Kyle as if he'd never seen him before, Danny reached up and touched him on the cheek. Then he pulled back his hand as if he shouldn't have done it. He watched Kyle a minute, then doubled up his fist and punched him lightly on the shoulder.

''I'm working on my swing, Mr. Rivers,'' he said, hoping this would be all right in case touching Kyle on the face wasn't.

''I'm not Mr. Rivers, I'm your dad.''

''You mean I can call you 'Dad'?''

''I reckon so,'' Kyle said.

Danny suddenly saw several boys from school. His eyes danced when he looked back at Kyle, and his voice tumbled out in excited jabbers:

"Can I tell them? Can I tell them you're my real, live dad and you just found me?" His tone was full of a joy that Kyle had never heard in anyone before.

"Yes, you can tell them, son."

Danny spun round and began to run. Then he stopped so suddenly that he almost stumbled. "Can I have a dog again?"

"Yes, you can have a dog."

Kyle stood and looked at Karen's questioning eyes. She had been silent, too happy at what she had witnessed to break in on any part of it. His dream had come true, and she loved life for giving it to him, but now she wondered if what she had seen in Kyle's eyes had been only love for his son.

"I'm so happy for you, Kyle," she said, searching his eyes, hoping to see what she'd seen. Suddenly it was there again, gazing down at her. "Oh, Kyle," she murmured.

He took her in his arms and kissed her. Again he kissed her.

"After I left you last night," he said, "I did some serious thinking, but I still didn't change my mind about staying until Danny managed to open my eyes right after sunup. I took the job of deputy sheriff this morning."

"Then you'll be staying," she said, smiling broadly.

"Yes, I reckon I've got a steady job. But there was something else I had made up my mind to do this morning after I picked you up. It got postponed when Julian sent me to Bolden's." Kyle's gaze traveled over her lovely face. Then his eyes came to rest on hers. "I wanted to tell you that I love you." Kyle felt her melt against him with a muffled sob. Her arms slipped up around his neck and she pressed her face against his. "And now that you know that," he continued, "will you marry me?"

She was nodding, but unable to speak the word. Last night she had thought she would lose him, but today he was speaking of a lifetime together for them. Reluctantly, she let go of him, and having regained her composure with a great effort, she stepped back and looked up at him.

"Yes, Mr. Rivers, I would be very, very proud to marry you," she said, trembling with excitement.

"Tomorrow?" he asked.

"Well, no, I cannot marry you until spring, when school is out. I couldn't just walk out on them."

"I'd let you teach until next spring."

"I wouldn't be able to teach one day after I became your wife," she said, her eyes alive with happiness.

"How come?"

"Because I intend to be a better wife than I am a teacher, and I'm the best teacher in the territory!"

She laughed and snuggled into his beckoning arms. He kissed her, then drew away with a thoughtful look.

"I wasted many years on the chance of a dream coming true. I reckon I can wait until spring on a promise like that."

"Are you and Miss McLaughlin sweethearts now, Dad?"

Kyle looked down and saw Danny and his friends only a few feet away. Then he looked back into Karen's eyes.

"Are we sweethearts?" he asked, controlling a grin.

"Yes, sweetheart," Karen said.

Kyle studied Danny again. "Yes, son, I reckon we're sweethearts."

"Yep," Danny said, puffing out his chest in importance as he turned toward the other boys. "They're sweethearts and they even like each other!"